Ladies and Gentlemen,
THE *B*IBLE!

Ladies and Gentlemen,
THE BIBLE!

Jonathan Goldstein

RIVERHEAD BOOKS
New York

RIVERHEAD BOOKS
Published by the Penguin Group
Penguin Group (USA) Inc.
375 Hudson Street, New York, New York 10014, USA
Penguin Group (Canada), 90 Eglinton Avenue East, Suite 700, Toronto, Ontario M4P
2Y3, Canada (a division of Pearson Penguin Canada Inc.)
Penguin Books Ltd., 80 Strand, London WC2R 0RL, England
Penguin Group Ireland, 25 St. Stephen's Green, Dublin 2, Ireland
(a division of Penguin Books Ltd.)
Penguin Group (Australia), 250 Camberwell Road, Camberwell,
Victoria 3124, Australia (a division of Pearson Australia Group Pty. Ltd.)
Penguin Books India Pvt. Ltd., 11 Community Centre, Panchsheel Park,
New Delhi—110 017, India
Penguin Group (NZ), 67 Apollo Drive, Rosedale, North Shore 0632,
New Zealand (a division of Pearson New Zealand Ltd.)
Penguin Books (South Africa) (Pty.) Ltd., 24 Sturdee Avenue, Rosebank, Johannesburg
2196, South Africa

Penguin Books Ltd., Registered Offices: 80 Strand, London WC2R 0RL, England

This is a work of fiction. Names, characters, places, and incidents either are the product of
the author's imagination or are used fictitiously, and any resemblance to actual persons, living or dead, business establishments, events, or locales, is entirely coincidental. The
publisher does not have any control over and does not assume any responsibility for author
or third-party websites or their content.

Some of these stories were previously broadcast or published in slightly different form as
follows: "Adam and Eve," "Cain and Abel," and "My Troubles" on *This American Life*; "The
Tower of Babel," "Noah's Ark," "The Golden Calf," and "King David," parts one and two,
on CBC Radio's *WireTap*; "Samson and Delilah" in *The Walrus* magazine.

Copyright © 2009 by Jonathan Goldstein
Cover design by Benjamin Gibson
Cover photo by Lori Nix
Book design by Tiffany Estreicher

First Riverhead trade paperback edition: April 2009

Library of Congress Cataloging-in-Publication Data

Goldstein, Jonathan, date.
  Ladies and gentlemen, the Bible! / Jonathan Goldstein.—1st Riverhead trade pbk. ed.
    p. cm.
  ISBN 978-1-59448-367-7
  1. Bible—History of Biblical events—Fiction. I. Title.
  PR9199.4.G64L33 2009
  813'.6—dc22

                                        2008051491

PRINTED IN THE UNITED STATES OF AMERICA

10 9 8 7 6 5 4 3 2 1

ALSO BY JONATHAN GOLDSTEIN

Lenny Bruce Is Dead

For Heather

And in memory of my grandparents:
Bookie, Lily, Moe, and Sam

Contents

Preface: Inside the Grey Derby 1

Adam and Eve 13

Cain and Abel.. 26

Noah and the Ark.. 44

The Tower of Babel.. 66

Jacob and Esau.. 79

The Golden Calf... 115

Samson and Delilah.. 129

King David.. 155
    Part I: Goliath.. 155
    Part II: Bathsheba 170
    Part III: Absalom.. 186

Jonah and the Big Fish.. 200

My Troubles (A Work in Progress, by Joseph of N—) ... 230

Ladies and Gentlemen,
THE *B*IBLE!

Inside the Grey Derby

By anyone's standard their family was Jewish, but they played by their own rules. While they did not keep the Sabbath, they did go to synagogue on Yom Kippur. They begged God to forgive their sins and inscribe them in the Book of Life. They did so while glancing at their watches every ten minutes. They did not speak Hebrew, but they did toss around a few Yiddish words, half of which were made up, such as the grandmother's word for the TV remote, something she called "der pushkeh." They did not study Torah, but they did watch *The Ten Commandments* every year on TV. Even when the long journey through the desert became unendurable, they stuck it out. They believed enough for that.

There were certain restaurants they went to, not because they were kosher, but because they were "kosher-style." Kosher-style was like the apartment across the hall from kosher, and whereas keeping kosher required rigorous observation of rules, keeping kosher-style required only a Jerusalem napkin holder on the table and the restaurant's name written out front in large Hebraic calligraphy.

Growing up, there was a restaurant they went to on Friday nights. It was called the Grey Derby and among the Jews of their town it was very popular. More popular than other kosher-style restaurants like Schneider's—essentially a living room with a cash register where one learned it was time to go when Mr. Schneider walked out of the bathroom in his boxer shorts, a toothbrush in his mouth. The other competitor was Spaghettiville, a basement operation they never went to, assuming it to be like Margaritaville, but with spaghetti.

They were a big group—a large family of uncles, aunts, great-aunts, sons-in-law, and a man named Goldberg whom no one was sure how they knew, and the Derby was their place. Never mind it was so crowded on Friday nights that you were guaranteed a half-hour wait—and never mind it wasn't even a line you waited in. They were crammed into a kind of holding cell at the entrance, shoulder to shoulder, becoming impossibly, ferociously—supernaturally—hungry, the waft of veal and kishke slowly driving them mad.

They always got the same table—a long one in back, by the bathrooms. Once seated, they started in on whatever was left over by the previous diners.

"They hardly even touched the challah rolls," the mother would say, looking around for leftover chopped liver to spread.

It didn't take them more than ten minutes to devour their own weight in boiled chickens, stewed chickens, chickens in baskets, flanken, kishke, and a spicy fat called "speck" that has since been made illegal. Then they were on to the next event: the check. They were not a family disposed to acts of athleticism, but the fight for the bill was, for them, a kind of spiritual-emotional sport.

"I swore on my life I'd pay," the mother would say and, quick like a cat, she'd claw the bill from the table and stick it down her blouse. Swearing upon her own life was a big move of the mother's in those days. To her way of thinking it allowed the grandfather to know in no uncertain terms that should he pay, God would strike his daughter dead in the parking lot. Still, her oath did not keep the uncle, a man named Nat, from reaching into the neck of the mother's shirt while yelling, "It's a man's privilege."

Their table sat below a wall-length mural of David in the midst of slaying Goliath—the moment the rock was colliding with Goliath's forehead. That was their backdrop—Goliath going down. It was of pretty amateurish quality, probably painted by one of the owner's kids, but there was something about it that captured the young son's imagination. As he sat there nibbling bowling ball–sized verenikas, he gazed, self-satisfied, at the ultimate image of the little-Jew-who-could.

Reclining back into their booth, their belt buckles undone, and their braggadocio about how much they'd eaten fading into silence, the young boy stared up at the mural, and subjected his father to a barrage of questions. It was always the same: How old was David when he slew Goliath? How much did God help him slay Goliath? When it comes to slaying, why use a sling?

The father listened attentively, easing back farther

into his seat. Were he a smoker, he would have lit his pipe with a thoughtful look on his face, but as he was not a smoker, he picked his teeth with a salad fork.

"David was no older than you are," he said, "but even at such a young age, the kid had a sense of showmanship. Sure, he could have snuck into Goliath's tent and brained the sleeping giant with some heavy piece of ancient pottery, but where's the glory in that? No, the Jew's way is to give things a little razzle-dazzle—to give the angels something to talk about. Now the sling had just been invented and most people were put off by its newness, preferring the old-fashioned ways of murdering—a stab to the stomach, a bludgeon to the skull. But not the Jews. We were always a nation of early adapters. Monotheism. Liquid soap. We shrug our shoulders and say, 'why not?' and it is that shoulder-shrugging spirit that's helped us survive."

The father was not a religious man. Aside from once trying to teach the boy the Hebrew alphabet through rhyme—"Aleph, bais, give me a raise. Ress, tess, kiss my ess"—and trying to get the boy to start calling him Tateh after having just watched *Fiddler on the Roof*, Yiddishkeit just wasn't his thing. He was never one for synagogue, complaining about the hard wooden pews, the incomprehensibility of the Hebrew language, and the way that synagogue, rather than inspiring him, made him feel as though he were being suffocated in a claustrophobic coffin that reeked of old-man smell.

But talking about the Bible was something else. Its heroes were like superheroes or Greek gods—but better yet, they had really existed. And not only that—they were even distant relatives! The father, who hadn't even spoken to his own brother in years, took all of this in stride, but the boy did not. He couldn't see how you could. He had hundreds of questions, and each one spawned more.

"Didn't Goliath have friends to avenge his death?" he asked.

"What friends? Goliath was a bully and a blowhard," the father said. "I've always imagined him as a giant version of that guy who used to share my desk at the insurance office. Ian something. Now David, he was a good kid, but he made mistakes and God had to teach him right from wrong—by smiting his children and such."

In the father's retellings, it often seemed that God was no friend to the Jews. Not like Nixon, whom the family still adored for having delivered bombs to Israel's doorstep during the Yom Kippur War.

Staring up at the mural, he explained that, in those days, they beheaded vanquished giants. "But try putting a picture of that on a wall and you'll have the Board of Health up your ass in two seconds."

From David they veered into Genesis.

"Were there unicorns in Eden?" the boy asked.

"There were," the father said, "but God had to kill them to punish man." The father explained how, as an added penalty, "God commanded Adam and Eve to murder the unicorns themselves and so they wandered the Earth, strangling unicorns as they wept."

"How horrible," the boy said. "How could someone kill a unicorn—even if God told you to?"

"In the beginning, it was rough on them but they got used to it, making small talk as they strangled. In the end it actually brought them closer and helped their marriage. Don't worry. God knows what he's doing."

From Genesis, they wound their way further back still, eventually arriving at the very beginning. Before the beginning. The beginning of everything—even God. It always struck the boy as a very commonsensical question: if God created everything, who created God? He didn't understand why the question wasn't foremost on everyone's mind. On the very first page of the

7

illustrated children's Bible he had at home, God was already there. He would flip backward, to make sure he hadn't missed anything, but there was only a table of contents. It crossed his mind that the pages dealing with that prebeginning might have fallen out. A lot of the pages were lost, so when he went to his grandparents', he looked in their Bible—they kept it beside the phone book—but it was the same story: "In the beginning, God created the Heavens and the Earth." No prequel. Nothing.

As the waiter began the arduous task of clearing the table of empty plates, glasses, oily napkin balls, and ashtrays filled with olive pits and tiny bones, the boy asked his father, "Who's God's god?"

"God is beyond time," he said. "God created time. To ponder this too hard can drive the average man to insanity. Let us instead ponder dessert." Complimentary lemon tea and coffee was brought forth with a tray of rice pudding and baked apples. The boy could not understand how anyone could eat when such huge questions hung in the air—though to be fair, he could also not understand how anyone could eat after having just ingested a barn's worth of meat and chicken. How could someone invent time? That was like inventing dreaming or darkness.

"What was God doing all those millions of years just floating around all by himself in the nothingness all day?"

"He was lonely," the father said. "He had no choice but to make us. Of course he didn't get it right out the gate. It took a few tries."

The father then went on to list the universes that preceded their own.

"Before this one, there were incomplete universes that did not please the Almighty. Some were too cluttered—with daybeds and piles of blankets all over the place making even the beach smell musty and close. Other universes of just one person—a man named Morris who sat in a room by himself, trying to decide whether to cuff his pants or let them drag. And can you imagine the delicate touch it took to create free will? No, I'm sure those early universes were filled with marionette people getting their strings tangled up in each other. Universes of tangled string! Universes of nothing but light! Universes that were perfect in every way but were missing the right support beams and so collapsed after only five seconds. But what a spectacular five seconds they might have been."

Spotting a chicken wing bone, gnawed clean, poking out from under a place mat, he went on, inspired.

"Universes where bridges and buildings were made of chicken bones, but chicken bones did not come from chickens. They were grown from chicken bone seeds and chicken bone seeds came from boiling tears because tears tasted like chicken soup! Chicken soup came from chicken soup rain clouds and chicken soup rain coats were made of feathers and instead of carrying umbrellas people carried ladles."

After a meal like that, how his father could even *think* of chicken—let alone conjure a universe of poultry—boggled the boy's mind and made him slightly nauseous.

"So why didn't God mention any of this in the preface?"

The father waved his hand. "Who reads prefaces? A person's job on Earth is to make the best sense of things that he can. Not to give up and live like an animal, but not to get too hung up on the details. Look at the hamantasch." A hamantasch was a prune-filled triangular cookie eaten on Purim and the father was often turning to it for guidance. "Depending on whose version you believe, it either symbolizes the evil Haman's triangle-shaped hat or Haman's dirty triangle-shaped ears. Either way, they go good with coffee."

The idea of eating a pastry made to replicate the salient facial feature of a Jew-hating mass murderer struck the boy as sick—like eating a licorice Hitler mustache—but the father's point had been made, though many years later when thinking back upon it, the boy would be hard-pressed to say what exactly that point was.

When the bill had been settled, their belt buckles refastened, and the younger sister awoken from under the table, they commenced their walk to the door, the grandfather shaking hands as he went, the uncle handing out business cards. At the entrance, they smiled with compassion at the new crowd of hungry Jews who awaited their turn, and in the parking lot they smoked cigars, chewed mints, jingled car keys, and got into political arguments that devolved into finger pointing, foot stomping, and the shouting of names like turkey, schmo, schmendrick, and schmegeggy. They enjoyed each other's company and took their time parting. After all, it was only five thirty and the whole night lay ahead.

Adam and Eve

In the beginning, when Adam was first created, he spent whole days rubbing his face in the grass. He picked his ear until it bled, tried to fit his fist in his mouth, and yanked out tufts of his own hair. At one point he tried to pinch his own eyes out in order to examine them and God had to step in.

Looking down at Adam, God must have felt a bit weird about the whole thing. It must have been something like eating at a cafeteria table all by yourself when a stranger suddenly sits down opposite you, but it is a stranger you have created, and he is eating a macaroni salad that you have also created, and you have been sitting at the table all by yourself for over a hundred billion years; and yet still, you have nothing to talk about.

It was pitiful the way Adam looked up into the sky and squinted.

Before He created Adam, God must have been lonely; now He was still lonely, and so was Adam.

Then came Eve.

Since the Garden of Eden was the very first village, and since every village needs a mayor as well as a village idiot, it broke down in this way: Eve: mayor; Adam: village idiot.

Sometimes, when Adam would start to speak, Eve would get all hopeful that he was about to impart something important and smart, but he would only say stuff like: "Little things are really great because you can put them in your hand as well as in your mouth."

Eve would often ponder how one minute she was not there or anywhere, and now she was. Adam would ponder nothing. When she closed her eyes at night, Eve knew that the blackness was all things at once. In her dreams she danced in the tops of trees. Her beautiful thoughts flew out her ears and lit up the sky like fireflies, and there were all kinds of people to talk to and hug. And then she would hear snoring. She would wake up, and there would be Adam, his yokel face pressed right against hers, his dog food breath blowing right up her nostrils.

Eve stared up at the sky. Adam draped his arm across her chest, and brought his knee up onto her stomach. God, watching in Heaven, must have feared for Adam's broken heart as though the whole universe depended on it.

Adam was close to the animals and spent all day talking to them. Except for God, Eve had no one.

She would complain to the Lord any chance she got.

"Adam is a nimrod," she would say, and the Lord would remain silent.

God was the best and all that, and she loved the hell out of him, but when it came to trash talk, he was of no use.

Adam was constantly trying to impress her.

"Look what I have made," he said one bright morning, his hands cupped together.

Eve looked into his hands then she pulled away and shrieked. Adam was holding giraffe feces.

"I've sculpted it," said Adam. "It is for the Lord."

He opened his smelly hands wide to reveal to her a tiny little giraffe with a crooked neck.

On some days, Adam galloped about exploring. His hair was wiry and when it got sweaty it hung in his eyes. Adam was cute this way. On one such day, he saw a snake. Adam made the snake's acquaintance by accidentally stepping on his back.

"Boy, that smarts," said the snake, smiling through the mind-numbing pain.

Adam lifted him from off the ground and brought him up to his face to see him better.

Their eyes locked, and in that very moment the snake concluded that, indeed, Adam was an oaf, and that as king of the Earth, his reign would very soon end. There was a new sheriff in town and it was he. It was no longer the story of Adam, but the story of the snake. He could tell all of this just by simply looking into the man's idiot eyes.

"I have seen you with another like you," he said to Adam, "but instead of the dead snake between the legs, she has chaos there."

"That's Eve," said Adam, all animated. "I named her that myself. God made her from out of my rib."

He showed the snake the scar on his side.

The snake looked at Adam in silence. The idea of Adam—Adam the schlemiel, Adam the fool—being God's favorite, was enough to give the snake a migraine.

"You aren't at all like I imagined," the snake said. "I thought you'd be closer to the ground . . . more pliant—greener. I tried to explain to God that to make you balanced up on your hind legs was architecturally unsound. I don't know why I bother."

Adam sat and listened wide-eyed. Eve hadn't the patience to sit and chat like this, so when the snake suggested they get into the habit of meeting every once in a while to talk, Adam was very excited to do so.

As they lazed on their backs staring up at the sky, the snake would brag about how he was older than the whole world and that he used to pal around with God in the dark, back before creation. He said that in the darkness, it was a truer, freer time, that in the darkness was the good old days. He told Adam that back in the very beginning, he had all kinds of thoughts on how to make the Garden of Eden a better place, but that God was just too stubborn to listen to reason.

"'Make the earth out of sugar,' I told him. 'Instead of stingers, give bees lips they can kiss you with.'"

The snake had opinions about everything. Often, he complained about the other animals. "The hyenas stole my pecans," he said. "The squirrels don't respect me. A zebra tried to kill me!"

Adam didn't always agree with the snake—in fact a lot of what he said went straight over his head—but there was still something about him that made him get into a very particular mood. He made the world feel bigger. Sometimes when Adam was with Eve, sitting there in icy silence, he would think to himself, "I sure could go for a good dose of snake."

Adam really loosened up with him, too, which made it all the more sad to watch the snake's duplicity. You would think that after all the time they spent together, the snake would find it within himself to start liking Adam, just a little bit, but instead, he only grew to hate him more.

He took to comforting himself with thoughts of Adam's wife, Eve. From what he heard from Adam, she was, as well as being hot, very smart. Often, he would imagine running into her and the instant synergy they would have.

"Adam neglected to tell me how leggy you are," he would say, wrapping himself around her calf.

The snake had no idea what he looked like. He was hairless, bucktoothed, four inches tall, and he spoke with a lisp. Adam had the IQ of a coconut husk, but he was still human. The snake, in his arrogance, was unable to grasp this, and so he daydreamed.

"Sometimes I'd think you were watching me," the snake imagined saying to Eve. "Because I felt like there were ribbons wrapped around me. I would turn around to catch you sneaking a peek from behind a tree, but all I'd see were the hedgehogs who mocked me."

On Eve's very first day Adam had explained to her the rules of the garden just the way God had explained them to him. He had lifted his head up and made his back stiff. He had spoken the way a radio broadcaster from the 1940s would. Another kind of woman, someone softer than Eve, might have found this charming. He explained that, except for the tree of knowledge, every tree in the garden was theirs to eat from.

"I am a fan of the pear," Adam said. "It is not unlike an apple whose head craves God."

"Tell me more about this tree of knowledge," said Eve. She enjoyed the sound of it. "The tree of knowledge." It sounded very poetic.

"There's not much to tell," said Adam. "If we eat from it, we will die."

From then on Eve talked about the tree of knowledge all the time. It was tree of knowledge this and tree of knowledge that. It was like it wasn't a tree at all, but a movie star. Sometimes she would just stand by the tree and stare at it. It was on such an occasion that she met the snake.

When Eve first caught sight of him, she brought her hand to her mouth and gasped. She had seen some repulsive animals in her day—a booby that percolated her vomit to just beneath her tonsils, a dingo that instilled in her a sublime sense of nature's cruelty, and a death-watch beetle that filled her with existential dread—but still, there was something about the snake that made her realize in a flash that the world was anywhere from sixty to eighty percent oilier than she would have ever imagined.

"Hi," said the snake. "In the mood for some fruit of knowledge? It's fruity."

"We were told not to eat from that tree, or else we would die," said Eve.

"Die! What an ignorant thing to say," said the snake, all chewing on a blade of grass in the side of his mouth. "If there is a trap door in paradise, then it is not really paradise, is it?"

The snake made interesting points. That appealed to Eve. He could see he was making an impression.

"All I'm saying is to give it a try. Many things will be made immediately clear to you once you partake. I can talk about it all day and you still won't get it. You have a right to at least try it, right? I'm not saying go out and eat an entire fruit. Have a nibble. A nibble isn't really eating, is it?"

Eve found arguing semantics exhilarating. But then she thought of what God would say and how he would say it.

"Thou hast disobeyed me," He would intone. There would be a lot of intoning.

She looked at the tree. The way the sun shone through its leaves was beautiful. Everything seemed to point to "Nibble the fruit."

Then the snake said: "Think about it. Does God want companions who can think for themselves, or does he want lackeys and yes-men? Wouldn't God want a few surprises? God's telling you not to eat the fruit was just a test to see if you could think for yourselves, to see if you could exist as equals to God. The day you taste the fruit is the day God will no longer be lonely. At least give it a lick."

Eve looked at the fruit. Then she looked at the snake. Then, slowly, she parted her lips and pushed out her tongue, all wet and warm and uncertain. She ran its tip along the smooth flesh of the fruit.

The snake smiled.

"Has anyone died?" he asked. "Now take a tiny little nibble. Just a speck. Just to see."

The fruit was squishy and tart. She smooshed it around in her mouth. She squinted her eyes.

It was a bit like trying on new glasses. It was a bit like an amyl nitrite popper. It was a bit like a big wet kiss on the lips right at first when you weren't sure if you wanted to be kissed or not. She felt a thousand little feet kicking at her uterus.

The idea of her own nudity, as well as Adam's, had always felt more like a Nordic, coed health spa thing; now, with the fruit of knowledge, it felt more like a Rio de Janeiro carnival thing. Her breasts felt like water balloons filled with blueberry jam and birds. Her nipples were like lit matchsticks. Her thighs, the way they swished against each other, were like scissors cutting through velour.

With her lips still glistening in tree of knowledge fruit juice, she ran off to find Adam. The snake watched her as he chewed on his slimy blade of grass and, as she receded into the distance, he thought something along the lines of "Now that's what I'm talking about."

"Kiss me, Adam," said Eve. "Taste my lips."

Adam, like any lummox truly worth his salt, could smell the minutest trace of knowledge coming his way, and thus he knew how to avoid it like the plague.

But yet there was also this: Eve had never sought

him out in the middle of the day before just to kiss him. It felt like a very lucky thing. When he took her in his arms, he told her that he loved her with his whole, entire heart.

He closed his eyes tightly and brought his lips to hers. Then he squinted. Then it started to rain and Eve began to cry.

During the darkest days ahead, with the fratricides and whatnot, Adam would often think back to his brief time in Eden. As he became an old man, he would talk about the garden more and more. A couple of times he had even tried to find his way back there, but he very soon became lost. He didn't try too hard anyway. He didn't want to bother God any more than he already had.

When Adam met someone he really liked, he would say, "I so wish you could have been there." It didn't seem fair to him that he was the one who got to be in Eden. "This sunset isn't bad," he'd say, "but the sunsets in Eden! They burned your nose hairs! They made your ears bleed!" He couldn't even explain it right.

"When you ate the fruit in Eden, it was like eating God," he would say. "And God was delicious. When you wanted Him you just grabbed Him." Now when he ate fruit, he could only taste what was not there.

But it wasn't all bad. After Eden, Eve became much gentler with Adam. After getting them both cast out, she decided to try as hard as she could to give Adam her love. She knew it was the very least she could do. She sometimes even wondered if that was why God had sent the snake to her in the first place.

Adam would tell his grandkids, his great-grandkids, and his great-great-grandkids about how he and Nana Eve had spent their early days in a beautiful garden, naked and frolicking, and the kids would say, "Eeyoo."

The children would swarm into the house like a carpet of ants. The youngest ones would head straight for Adam, lifting his shirt to examine his belly for the umpteenth time. They smoothed their hands across his flesh and marveled.

"Where's Grandpa's belly button?" they all asked. He stared at the children—they were all his children—and as they slid their little hands across his blank stomach, he wondered what it was like to be a kid.

Cain and Abel

On their first night outside the Garden of Eden, it was windy and cold and the air was full of whistling. They scraped at the tree trunks and dug their fingers into the earth. At the top of their voices, Adam and Eve called out to God.

"We get it," they screamed. *"You've made your point. Now let us back in, already."*

To fend off the cold, they hugged each other with all their might. They thought about all the things God had said in his wrath: how a little human would one day tear his way out of Eve, how they would no longer live forever, but would one day die. These thoughts made them colder. They slept face-to-face, pressed so tightly together that their noses hurt. Later they would learn to make clothing, but just then, all they had was each other. Nine months after that first night, this would change.

In the beginning, in the garden, a baby was supposed to be a surprise, appearing as suddenly as a sneeze. The way God intended it, two people in love would share a like-minded pretty thought, and then there it would be—a baby nesting in a tree above their heads. Or someone might lay a cheek upon someone else's stomach and simply feel happy to be alive, then would come the sudden weight of a baby upon the person's back. People would like this, too. It wouldn't be like they'd walk around afraid to have a good time for fear of making babies.

But the way God intended it did not pan out.

After He cast Adam and Eve out of the garden, God wed the creation of babies with the act of sex. It was like pairing the eating of a nectarine with a lunar eclipse, the tearing of a fig leaf with a sudden snowfall. Previously it had no inherent logic but since God made logic, now it was the way things would be.

On the night their child was born, Eve was asleep, dreaming about the ocean. She was swimming beneath it, breathing in the water like it was air. Very carefully, she climbed onto a shark and rode him.

I am actually doing it, she thought. Then the shark turned its head around and bit off her lower body.

Eve awoke suddenly. She had begun to give birth.

Adam hopped from foot to foot as Eve felt the pain crush her into the earth.

"There's a head sticking out of you," cried Adam, "and it has a face."

For a minute, Adam thought that this might be what a baby was: just a head that sticks out. He would just have to get used to it. But then, rather quickly, more came out. Shoulders, arms, tiny hands. Yes, this was the baby, and the baby was attached to a vine. After a few days, despite their great care, the vine wore away and baby Cain was freed into the world.

At the time of her second birth, there wasn't the same stage fright. Eve knew the drill. She laid herself on the ground and grabbed two fistfuls of grass.

Forty-three and a half hours later, Abel was born. They called Cain over to meet his new brother. They placed the baby in his arms. The baby was slippery and Cain lost his grip. Abel fell. He lay on the ground, looking up at his brother. He did not cry. Abel could not be rattled.

Back in those first days, things changed very quickly. A new person being born meant there was a giant spike in the population. For Cain, it made the planet feel lopsided. He watched Eve bounce the newborn in her lap and as she cooed at it, he felt the Earth's gravity tilt in their direction. It pulled at the insides of his stomach and made him seasick.

Years later, Adam and Eve would have many more children, but just then, there were only Cain and Abel. Because there was simply nobody else, the brothers became very close. They invented their own language and played each other's stomachs like snare drums. They butted their heads like goats and cracked each other's knuckles as though they were cracking their own.

They were different, though. Abel was a thinker. He thought about things: if he bit off his own pinkie toe, would it grow back? Cain, on the other hand, was a doer. He'd reel back his fist and break a donkey's nose for the sheer thrill of it all.

Because of their differing dispositions, Abel became a shepherd, which afforded him long hours of rumination as his sheep grazed, while Cain became a farmer, which allowed him to work with his hands.

Adam and Eve encouraged both their children to sacrifice a portion of their produce to the Lord.

"God told us to," said Adam, "and, considering what He could do to us, it's probably wise to obey."

When they were little, Cain and Abel did a pretty perfunctory job. They treated making sacrifices the way one would take to being forced to talk on the telephone to a crazy and infirm grandfather on his birthday.

"What does the Creator of the Universe need with cauliflower and dead sheep?" Abel would joke and Cain would laugh.

One day, when Adam and Eve thought the children were old enough, they sat them down and told the story of what life was like before they were born.

"In those days, God was like one of the family," said Adam.

Eve told Cain and Abel about "the screwup."

"What does it mean to die?" asked Cain.

"We're not exactly sure," said Eve. "But basically it means that one day—and this is not any day soon—we will no longer be."

There was silence, then Abel spoke up.

"If we won't be," he said, "then we won't even know that we're not being. There will be no we to see that we can no longer be, yes?"

"I guess that's true," said their mother. "Well put."

Abel smiled and went back to mashing a mutton liver that he was making into pâté for later.

Cain, on the other hand, felt like a sharp plum pit had been forcefully lodged down his throat. All his life he had felt like himself, that his hands and fingers—that his thoughts—were his own. Now he felt like they were someone else's, someone who could yank them away at any chosen moment. Until then, it had never even crossed his mind that such a thing could be possible.

*   *   *

31

The brothers continued to live their lives, but all the while Cain felt a new sadness. It was there all the time. It ate with him, worked with him, and in the morning it rose from his bed with him.

Dying! It just didn't make any sense. He knew this deep in his heart. He thought nothing was more important than making God change his mind—nothing. He began to take his sacrifices more seriously. They became elaborate and garish. They involved richly choreographed interpretive dances, colorful oblong facial masks, and the very best of his legumes.

But God never answered.

Cain started to change. When he got a splinter, he cursed the Heavens all out of proportion.

"Back in the Garden of Eden, there were no splinters," Cain said to Abel. "Instead of splinters they had trees that hung with fried eggs and home fries."

He even started to resent his parents. He spoke of them as though they had gambled away his inheritance.

"If it hadn't been for ignoramus number one tempting ignoramus number two, we'd be living in luxury!"

Cain tried to get Abel worked up about the whole thing, too, but Abel had an easy-come-easy-go-we-all-have-to-die-someday attitude that drove his brother crazy. As long as he had his sheep, as long as he could rub his naked feet through their wool, Abel felt that things were really not so bad.

Cain invented a game that he called Get the Hell Out of Eden. He always insisted on playing God.

"Get your naked asses out of here," yelled God.

"What? But we just got here," yelled Adam and Eve. "Maybe there's some kind of mistake."

"The Lord does not make mistakes."

God would then kick his brother in the ass. He would fall to the ground and, holding his ass, say, "Please, please have mercy on me, let's play something else," and God would laugh.

Now that he was older, every week Abel would choose the fattest, firstborn sheep and sacrifice them to God. Everything Abel did in life was for a reason—he ate so he would not be hungry, he made clothes so he would not be cold—but making sacrifices to God, he did it for reasons he could never know. He did it simply because he was told to. There was something about that that made him feel clean and deep.

Adam and Eve made their sacrifices out of fear of being further punished and Cain was pleading for answers and changes, but Abel fulfilled his obligation and walked away expecting nothing from God. Of all the people who'd been created, he was glad with the way things were, and God could not have helped liking that.

Meanwhile, Cain decided to test out a new approach with the Lord. He believed that God would have greater respect for him if he did not kowtow. *He's going to kill us!* he thought. He wanted God to understand that he couldn't walk all over people and then still have them come crawling back with their arms loaded up with gifts. No, they had to get tough. They had to show Him what was what. So Cain's sacrifices became more and more lackadaisical. He did not even check to see whether his gifts were being received or not. That would look like he was caving.

Then one day, while Cain was lying in a field, Abel came running over.

"God spoke to me," cried Abel.

Cain shot up and looked at his brother.

"What did he say?"

"He said he was a great fan of my sheep. He told me to keep up the good work."

"Was my name mentioned?" asked Cain.

"It didn't come up."

"What was it like to hear His voice?" asked Cain.

"Look at me," said Abel, "I'm still shaking."

There was a certain pang that Cain started to feel. It was in his stomach. He felt the pang grow sharpest when he looked upon his brother. He could hardly speak with him without having to hunch over in pain. Since the world was still new, and no one had yet felt this way, Cain did not know that it was jealousy he was feeling. Instead, he decided that his stomach no longer wanted to be his stomach. It wanted to escape his rib cage; it wanted to be Abel's stomach. This was because he wanted to be Abel. There was no shame in this. Being Abel meant being happy. Being Cain meant being wretched. Being Cain had brought him nothing.

He had a plan. He approached Abel with it. He decided to just spring it on him.

"I am no longer Cain," said Cain. "I am now Abel. We are both Abel."

"All right," said Abel.

The two Abels performed routines for the amusement of their brothers and sisters.

"How is that apple, Abel?"

"It is fine, Abel."

"Abel, could you pass it over so that I may have a bite?"

"I, Abel, don't see why not, Abel."

Then one day, things became more grave.

"If I am Abel," said Cain, "then I am just as much Abel as you yourself are Abel."

"I suppose that's true," said Abel.

"Before God are we not both Abel?" asked Cain.

"Well, in the case of being before God, I think at that time I would be Abel and you would go back to being Cain. At all other times, though, like when we're climbing trees, making pottage, and flirting with our sisters, you are just as much Abel as I myself am Abel."

"That won't do," said Cain. His eyes lingered on his brother. He looked at this other Abel as standing in the way of who he was. He was Abel. He knew this in his heart. He simply wanted it more.

When he heard his father call out for Abel and he saw his brother go forth, it made him feel like he was nothing. He couldn't even say that he felt like Cain anymore. One could not feel like Cain because it had no flavor. Cain was the absence of flavor. Cain was like saliva or a Wednesday.

This way God will have to show himself. This way God will have to stop playing possum and get directly involved in what is going on. These were Cain's thoughts.

Abel was among his flock when Cain neared him. Slowly, Cain pulled out his stick and slowly, he lifted it into the air. Still, though, there was no sign of God. He looked at the back of Abel's head. Then he looked into the sky. Just in case God was reading his mind, he thought to himself, *I'm really, really going to do it.*

He brought his stick down onto his brother's head; he could hear no sound at all. Abel just toppled over. He toppled over the way he did everything—with an easygoing acceptance. He sank to the earth, as though thinking, *I must fall, so I will fall. I am falling. I have fallen.*

Cain grabbed his brother by the shoulder and turned him over. His brother's eyes were wide open. It was like Abel was looking past him, over his shoulder and up into the sky. When they were kids, there was a game they played where Cain would do something, something bad, and Abel would look over just behind him, as though spying their father who'd been watching. Cain, full of fear, would slowly turn to meet his father's gaze. When he'd see that there was really no one there, he would laugh. It was like Abel was playing at their game, but this time, he did not move a muscle even to smile. Even when Cain pinched his cheek, pulling his face this way and that, his brother just lay there.

Here it was: death. Cain couldn't believe it. He'd been sure that at the last moment, God would step in. He would have thought that only God could have taken a person's life. But it was as simple as killing a sheep.

Abel, his eyes wide and unblinking, stared directly into the mystery of life and death, and he was not saying a word about any of it.

Cain sat back and waited. The sheep continued to graze and the sun continued to shine. There were no bolts of lightning, no booming voice from behind the clouds. Life went on.

*   *   *

That night, God appeared before Cain in a dream.

"Where is your brother?" asked God.

"It's always about my brother," said Cain. "Do you ever ask me where I am? No, that you don't think of."

"What have you done?" asked God. "Your brother's blood cries out to me from the ground."

"Am I my brother's keeper?" asked Cain.

God did not answer. He just gave him a look. It made Cain feel naked and small. He then felt the finger of God upon his forehead. It sank through his head and into his brain, where it spoke.

"The Earth shall scorn you," said the voice from the finger. "I shall scorn you. You will wander the Earth and death will not come. There will be no escape from your guilt. All will look upon you and none will dare kill you, for they will know you by your mark."

God withdrew his finger, leaving behind a fingerprint on Cain's forehead that was shaped like a teardrop. At first, he tried to convince himself that the mark was to protect him, that he had a secret pact with God, that they understood each other. For a while he would wake up in the morning and pretend to be immortal and famous, but he was not very good at pretending.

And so the Earth then did scorn him. Where once his hands withdrew berries and tomatoes, now they produced tobacco, ragweed, and alfalfa sprouts—things the world had never seen before.

So as the centuries passed, Cain abandoned farming and roamed the Earth. He walked with a sense of purpose, just in case anyone was watching, but in his heart he knew he had nowhere to go. He became so lonely and full of regret that instead of fearing death, he became yearnful of it. He would chase after bears, and they would scamper away.

"They haven't the balls," he'd say.

"Run, you little bitches," he'd call out to the tigers.

"Run, you yellow turd," he'd cry into the face of an alligator as he tried in vain to pry open its jaws.

More centuries passed, and Cain's desire for death became nearly constant.

He came to understand what jealousy was and he saw

it everywhere. The grass was jealous of the trees, the trees were jealous of the butterflies, the butterflies were jealous of the birds. Cain was jealous of all of them for their ability to die.

He would think about Abel, flying through the clouds on God's shoulders while he was left to futz around for hundreds of years, begging his own children to drive tree branches through his heart.

In life, Cain had been jealous of his brother; but it was in death that he became more jealous than he ever thought was possible.

He would feel Abel up there, looking down on him.

"You should see the look on your face," he would hear his brother say. "Trying to be all serious. You look like a gorilla."

Over time, Cain could no longer remember very much at all. Twenty years after the death of his brother, it seemed like it was only yesterday, but after two hundred years, it felt like something that might have happened in a dream. There were details he remembered that now seemed improbable, like the way he saw his brother's soul leave his body, and the way it waved good-bye to him and winked.

After three and then four hundred years, it all felt so long ago that who he was back then felt like someone else. When people he met asked him questions about the old days he just made stuff up.

"We had wings," he said.

They would ask him what Adam was like, and he would say that he was strict. Other times he would say he was jolly, that he loved his children.

After five hundred years, his story was repeated so often, that he only remembered the repeating, not the events themselves. It sounded like a fable, something that might have just as easily happened to an ass and a weasel as to himself and his brother. He began to doubt everything. He even began to wonder whether he had ever actually heard God's voice, whether the mark on his forehead was the mark of God and not just another liver spot. Was this a part of his punishment, he wondered, to be left so uncertain of whether God really was, or whether God was only something inside his own head? As he wandered, he met many people who had never talked to God, and who seemed unsure if

God existed, and he thought how things had changed since he was a boy.

After seven hundred years, when he told his story to himself, or heard it told by others, he felt nothing. He was too old to feel guilt, or remorse, or anything. He didn't even miss his brother anymore. He wanted nothing from God. He wanted nothing from the world. The world was what it was and he didn't need it to change. And in this way, he'd finally gotten his wish: to be just like Abel.

And then God let him die.

Noah and the Ark

Contrary to what most people think, the years leading up to the Great Flood were actually quite joyful. The preflood generation saw that the random smitings, the slavery, and the backbreaking labor of the early days had left their forefathers bitter and hateful, and so they collectively resolved to live lives of greater ease. Work, they realized, was overrated. Two days of toil a week were plenty—and this way, they had time for hobbies! People drew pictures, played music, and danced. It was a golden age of art, and the preflood generation really felt like they were on to something.

One man, though, felt that this whole business was

ass-backwards and off track. His name was Noah. He was over six hundred years old and was used to the work ethic of the good old days. He had lived long enough to see that craftsmanship was going down the toilet and he vowed never to become one of the "dancing dummies."

Not that he had much of a choice in the matter. Noah did not have any artistic inclination. He could not draw nor could he sing—and when he attempted to dance, he moved as though he were being pelted with apples. On the odd occasion on which he attempted to execute a jig, people would ask him if he had just stepped on something pointy, or if he was in need of the toilet. Then they would laugh.

Noah swore in his wrath that he, for one, would always remain old-school—and he would keep his children old-school, by teaching them about the value of good, hard work.

In those early days, people lived lives that were much longer than the puny ones we have now. It was possible for a man to live hundreds of years, and because of this, people matured at a much slower rate. Oftentimes, it took them a hundred years just to get going—to figure out what they wanted to be when they grew up. It was customary for children to live with their parents until they were married and, usually, marriage only occurred well after one had reached the century mark. This meant Noah had many years to instruct his children in the folly and danger of the lazy world around them. It also meant, for his children, a century of curfews, groundings, and slaps upon the head for finishing the last of the jellies. They lived by Noah's law—his wife and three sons, Shem, ninety-five, Japheth, ninety-three, and Ham the baby, eighty-seven.

Noah and his sons were contractors. They built huts for people. Officially, the company name was Noah & Son & Son & Son, though in private, Noah referred to his outfit as "Noah and the Dummies." He called his sons dummies at least a hundred times a day. There were worse names he could use—babbling Assyrian, locust thighs, harlot of the hills—but for his sons, "dummy" stung the worst—especially when there were girls around.

Noah saw the chain of command this way: God, the angels, Noah, his wife, his poodle Brandy, "the brothers

Dummy," and then the tools they built houses with. He was not sure where the nails went on the chain, but the idea of placing them below his sons did not gibe with his sense of justice. When his wife said that he was being cruel, too hard on the boys, he would say that he was just being honest. At such times he referred to himself as "Mr. Reality."

Noah knew he disciplined his boys with great ferocity, but he also knew it was a necessity. During those dark, evil days one had to teach one's children right from wrong, and if that involved the use of strops, riding crops, thick branches, throat punches, and leg locks, so be it. Without his brand of tough love, he feared they'd end up eating daisies and making out with dolphins. He was not going to be a sentimental old idiot. He was going to prepare his sons for a life of righteousness and hardship. That was what a father had to do.

"When I die and they must head the household, they will see that the injustice and folly of the world will beat them down far worse than my mouth, feet, and fists of wrath ever could. I will not be around forever."

Noah would spend hours soliloquizing about his lost youth and impending death. It would get his sons all revved up, licking their chops and dreaming of their future release.

"Ah, youth," Noah would say, all moist-eyed on a wine drunk, "ye has passed on like the fickle bitch-goddess that doth tickle the feet as she lops off the legs. Where once whipped my masculine mane of thick hair now lies the age-spotted dome of a deathbed sickie. Ah, me! The worms are readying themselves to crawl through my eye sockets! How can I venture out to the crocodile fights stinking of geriatric ointment?"

The thing was, though, that Noah wasn't anywhere close to dying. He was already six hundred years old and his stropping arm was as strong as that of a man half his age. When he landed his thick leather lash upon the calves of his sons they knew of his presence.

Noah sometimes thought back to the beatings his own father had doled out. Lamech was a giant of a man, with a beard you could climb and swing from like a jungle vine. When he was drunk, he paid neighboring boys to plant kicks in his ribs and stomach. Pain was the only thing that was real in life, Lamech would say. He saw the kicks as an invitation to meditate on the true essence of the universe. As the blood leaked from his mouth and navel, his face wore an expression of beatitude. Noah held the image of that face in his heart with the kind of nostalgic warmth that his countrymen only felt when remembering the birth of their children.

One day Noah heard a voice. He could only hear it faintly, under his own words. At first he thought it was a whistling in his nose hairs. He pressed a finger to each side of his nose and shotgunned mucus onto the ground, but still the ghostly voice below the surface of his speech persisted. When he stopped to try to hear it better, the little voice would cease. Noah looked at his sons. Had it been them, bad-mouthing him in whispers under their breath?

But their lips did not move. Noah started to speak once more, and once more he heard the tiny voice behind his own voice. It was mumbly and high-pitched and he could hardly hear it. He kept his mouth shut for the rest of the day, communicating his wishes to his sons through a hardy assortment of lashes, sucker punches, and cold stares. He put down his wine jug and waited for sobriety to return, whereupon he would take a long walk with Brandy, his beloved poodle. He would talk freely. He would see if the little voice still lingered.

Several weeks went by and the voice continued still. Eventually, Noah began to understand little bits, here and there. Out in the woods, Noah would speak:

"I am talking. I am talking. Blah blah blah. My sons are dummies. Blah blah blah. I am listening and I'm talking. Blah blah blah."

And as he spoke he could hear:

"You must build an ark made of gopher wood. I will guide your hand to choose animals which you will place within the ark. There is going to be a great flood. All will drown except you and yours and the chosen animals."

The little voice inside his nose pretty much always said the same thing. It instructed him to build a great ark, with various specifications and cubit requirements.

Noah had many questions, like "What's an ark?" and "Does one listen to the voice inside one's nose?"

Unfortunately for Noah, he had no one to share these problems with, and so he wandered the forests with Brandy, racking his brain for answers.

For increased clarity, Noah decided to stop drinking and take up a strict regimen of health food and exercise. He ate pine cones with strong, forceful bites and when he lashed his sons' calves, he did so using his left arm in equal portion to the right, favoring neither, so that they could both grow equally strong.

With his increased strength, the pip-squeaky voice, too, became stronger. He would ask it questions and it would answer him. It would answer him as he was asking the questions.

"What is a cubit?"

"It is the distance from your elbow to the tip of your long finger."

"What is gopher wood?"

"It's this wood that gophers like."

"How long will it take to build an ark?"

"Who knows?"

"Can I enlist the help of the Dummies?"

"No. You must do it yourself."

"Why build an ark?"

"I shall bring a flood that will wipe out the world.

The whole thing was a bad mistake. Except for you. You I like."

"Who are you?"

"I am the Creator of the Universe."

Upon hearing that, Noah's sinuses became as hollow as an empty conch, and from up within his nostrils there flowed a stream of blood.

Noah decided to sit the whole family down and tell them what God had in store.

"I was just talking with the Lord," said Noah. "And you know what? He regrets having made his children, too. 'They are all dummies, dear God,' I pleaded in the world's defense. 'What can a couple of regular guys like you and me do?' Then He says to me, He says—and He says it just like this—'I will blot them out.'"

The brothers looked at each other.

"What does that mean, 'blot them out'?" asked Shem.

"You take your thumb and push them into the earth like ladybugs! He's going to drown the whole world with his tears of rage, and after everyone's dead, he's going to start fresh. And guess who he chose to spearhead the operation? That's right. Me. Also, you virginal dummies have to get married so we can reseed the Earth. Enough waxing the nimrod! Clean your toga, balm your whip welts, and get out there!"

Regardless of how mentally imbalanced they might have felt their father to be, once Noah started building his ark, his sons felt great relief, as it kept him out of their hair. Noah said God would not allow anyone to help him, so he left his sons alone. No matter how long it took, he had to build the whole thing himself.

"Are you sure I can't do anything?" asked Shem. He loved the sound of his father turning down free labor and couldn't get enough of it.

"Are you a stupid dummy, you stupid?" his father would ask. "What did I just say? I'm the only one who can handle the job. Building an ark is man's work. Do you want to befoul the whole thing? If you so much as pound in one nail the whole thing is good only for the crapper."

His father had had visions before, and so the prevailing opinion was that the old man was, once again, off his rocker. There was the time he had drunk two and a half jugs of apricot wine and had become convinced a pile of rotted tree bark was imploring him to go live among goats. There was another time, sick in bed with a high fever, that he instructed his wife to climb up on the roof and yell out to God that he knew that sandals were for the weak of heart and from then on he and his sons would paint the soles of their feet with pepper sauce and keep stones between their toes.

Of everyone—the family, the neighbors, the village at large—it was Noah's youngest son, Ham, who was the only one who believed his father might not be crazy. From what Ham had heard about God, He was a lot like his father—tough, stubborn, and prone to yelling right in your face for pretty much no reason. A flood didn't seem that out of the question, and God would have chosen his father because his father felt just like He did: he hated his kids and was going to teach them the meaning of righteousness by killing them dead. If there was going to be someone God was going to get in touch with, to Ham, Noah seemed the obvious choice.

* * *

Sometimes, when his father was hard at work on his ark, Ham would sit off to the side and draw pictures of him. It incensed Noah.

"Are you sick in the head?" Noah would exclaim. "Why would anyone want to make stupid pictures? Can you eat them? Can you build a house with them? Can you use your precious art to diaper your loins?"

Noah wanted Ham to snap out of it, and he used reverse psychology to help him see his errors. He had seen how Ham spoke with his good-for-nothing artist friends and how his artist friends spoke back to him. He thought that if he talked their language, maybe he could get through to his son.

"Hey, jive turkey!" he said, approaching Ham. "That's right. Your old father Noah is going to be an artist from now on! How's that? Ha ha. Like this we can both make art and afterward we can talk about how deep it is. 'I pity the poor fool who can't dig art. You digging me, mister? Go ahead and make my day. Art is radical. Case closed.' Is that what you want? Well, I can't do it. Ach. Pteh. Yech."

As far as Noah could see, Ham's artist friends did not contribute much to society. Still, Ham liked them.

He spent much of his time with a woman artist named Lila. For her last piece, Lila had covered an apple tree in bear fur and replaced all the apples with dead snakes. She called it *The Tree of Knowledge*. Ham thought Lila's work was provocative, and he thought Lila herself was possessed of a strange, blond-haired weasel-like beauty.

It was while sitting together one day, sketching pictures of Noah as he worked, that Lila told Ham that she thought his father was the truest artist she'd ever met, and that his ark was his art.

"Think about it," she said. "He builds it for reasons no one can fathom, he applies himself to it every day, and every day he works with great passion."

Hearing Lila talk about his father that way while watching him work was enough to make Ham feel tenderly toward the old man.

Feelings of tenderness would cease as soon as his father opened his mouth.

"You'd better not be representing my likeness. And when I die, don't you dare make a mural that lovingly sings my praises. If you do some phony mural of me, I'll come back from the grave as a ghost and scream in your ear. 'What are you doing, you lousy good-for-nothing!'

I will screech. 'Also, use cross-hatching to make the side of my face more shrouded in dark.'"

Japheth and Shem had already taken for themselves brides. Ham had to find a mate for himself, too, lest he provoke his father's lash-heavy ire.

"If somehow the old man is right about this whole flood thing," said Ham, turning to Lila, "I'd like you to come ride out the flood with me."

Lila considered Ham's offer, then she took his hand.

"I suppose the new world will need artists," she said.

When the ark was ready, Noah took to the task of herding animals. After just one day of work, he looked like hell. He appeared to be bleeding out of every pore in his body. He had two black eyes, three broken ribs, and his nose hung half off from a bobcat bite. So great was his pain that, after that first day, even he began to doubt whether he had actually heard the voice of God.

"Maybe they are all right about me. Maybe I am sick in the head. But what is there left for me? If I admit to that, then I will be laughed out of town. The kids and the wife will make my domestic life a living hell. There is nothing left for me but to persist."

And so he persisted. He decided he would start small. He would collect the tiniest animals he could— ants, grasshoppers—and then slowly work his way up to squirrels and kittens.

"You should try to catch a hummingbird! That you should try," Noah complained to his wife. "Once you succeed in catching one, you hate it so much that you end up just strangling it. After three times you learn to control your temper, but that's still two dead hummingbirds and an entire morning's work shot to hell."

As Noah hunted around for animals, he judged them. He wanted to try to bring only the most worthy animals onboard his ark. He would stop by a group of rabbits and figure out who was a hardworking rabbit and who was a lazy, stupid dummy. Judging the rabbits made him feel a bit like God. He liked that.

"If I were you," he'd say, squatting beside a white bunny, "I'd eat facing a tree. As it is you look like a good-for-nothing layabout, but with that cabbage leaf in your mouth, you look like you have a secret agenda— a secret agenda you are too stupid a bunny to carry out."

As he walked away with the ones he had chosen for salvation, he would look back at their brethren and shake his head disapprovingly. "Good-bye, you dead dummies." And that was that.

For a long time, there was no rain, so Noah took to praying for it.

"Please, dear Lord who is a just lord, remember not our pact, kind Sire? I was to build the Boat of Heaven and You were to rain down the floods of Hell. I have kept my end of the deal, big strong oily-muscled One. Should it not flood I will appear as a stupid dummy before my family and friends. I have heeded the words from my nose, dear Lord my God, and now You must reek a flood upon the land so that we both do not appear as asses before the world. I will watch those stupid dummies drown from the safety of the Lord's ark and I will say, 'Ha. Look at you, you dumb stupids who heed not the Lord. Not so smart now, your lungs full of brine.'"

In this way, Noah conversed with the Lord, going on about how no one understood either of them, and how now, with the Lord's help, they will all see how stupid they are. They will see this for only a few minutes—an hour tops—and then they will drown. Noah imagined them all down there floating in the water like pickled lab rats—the butcher, still in his bloody apron, the lousy jerk who cut his hair and was always trying to convince him to grow out his bangs—the whole lot of them under the water, gasping for one last breath.

The flood started slowly. It did not seem biblical at all. The first day was nothing more than a drizzle, really, nothing to cause alarm. It continued like this for some time.

"We sure are getting an awful lot of rain for this time of year," people said, but eventually it got worse. The rain fell faster and heavier, each drop fat with purpose and spite.

Ham stood looking at the ark with Lila at his side. His father was already onboard. He had begun to live in there several days earlier as the very first drops of water fell. Ham turned his head toward the sky and felt the drops of rain pockmark his face.

He imagined them all in the ark. He imagined the aardvarks, the orangutans, the smell, the claustrophobia—his father's constant screams and shouts. He imagined himself deciding at the very last minute to forgo the ark entirely and take his chances with the flood. At the very last minute, when they were all loaded inside, he would offer to go back out and close the door behind them. Unless Noah had already trained a monkey for the task, someone would have to do it.

"I must sacrifice myself so that you may live," he would say.

"You dumb, stupid dummy," his father would answer. "God is going to close the door. Stop being melodramatic and go clean the hyena cage."

The sky began to hemorrhage. All at once, the drops became indistinguishable one from the other. The water poured down like all the heavens had become an inverted ocean. Ham opened his mouth to scream and caught a yapful of water. The taste reminded him of the time when he was ten and almost drowned at the beach. In a panic, he grabbed Lila by the skin of her bicep and together they ran up the plank and into the cold, echoey darkness of the ark.

*   *   *

The first hands he heard banging at the outside walls felt like nails pushing into his temples. Then there were more hands. Pounding. Punching. Scratching. Then kicks and shrieking that even drowned out the sound of the rain.

The worst was when Ham could make out individual voices. He could hear their neighbor Zebeleh and her little daughter Ariel.

"You know we could empty out the alligator cage, to make room for a few more people," offered Ham. "The world can do without alligators."

"And disobey God, you dummy?—and you try reopening that door. Do you have any idea what a pain in the ass we'd be in for? No, thanks."

Noah sat down and ate apples in the dark, waiting for his ark to rise above the world.

For forty days and forty nights they rode the ark as the animals roared, whined, and screeched. Sometimes, when things quieted down, Noah and his family pressed their ears against the walls to try to figure out where they were. Sometimes they tried to imagine what all of this looked like to the fish. Were the fish allowed to live because they were more pious than everyone else? Was the secret to piety keeping your mouth shut?

Sometimes Noah tried to get his family to sing to help uplift their spirits, but their songs would usually degenerate into sobs and cries and Noah would stomp off, disgusted with the boatload of them. Most often, though, they just spent their time remembering. Ham thought back to the days he'd spent with his artist friends and some of the old crowd he ran with. You couldn't put down your money purse in front of Olgar without having him riffle through it and help himself to a few coins to disperse to the poor; but when he did his imitation of a one-armed dwarf milking a large cow, he could make Ham laugh like nobody else. And there was Alois, who lived in a tree house and made big pots of bark soup for the hungry; and Gwendolyn, a young widow who kept her big fat baby in a sack on her back and could dance with so much joy that to see her, you couldn't help but smile. He thought about every single person he had ever known, and how he would never see them again.

Thinking it might bring him some solace, Ham pulled out a stick of his sketching coal and some parchment and went over to draw the puppies in their cages. He studied their faces. He tried to see what God and his father had seen in them, why they had chosen these particular dogs over all the others. On the surface, they looked no different from any other puppies he had ever seen. They were small and furry.

The two dogs paced about their cage, and, as Ham watched them, the puppy that was slightly larger suddenly set upon the haunch of the other and, for no apparent reason, tore into it with nasty, purposeful bites. The smaller dog yelped, twisted its body over, and sank its teeth into the ear of its attacker. Locked upon each other in this way, the puppies rolled across the floor, their eyes glowing an unearthly purple.

Ham turned away and walked over to the giraffe cage. There he found the long-necked beasts eye to eye, each trying to step on the other's hooves. Up near the roof, their mouths were opened wide, crying out in silence. He looked over at the tiger cage, where the tigers were scraping at the walls to get at the bear cubs next door, and the bear cubs sat stock-still, eyeing Ham with hunger.

Ham left the cages and went looking for Lila. She was sitting on the floor, painting a flower onto a rock she held in her hand. He knelt down beside her, put his face in her hair, and waited for the rain to stop.

The Tower of Babel

After the flood, man's relationship with God changed. Where once there was disinterest—a sort of "you go your way, we'll go ours" attitude—there was now distrust. The generations after Noah did not know when their time might come to be wiped out.

Noah had said the people of the Earth were evil, that God had to get rid of them and start over, that God had made some kind of mistake—either in killing them or in creating them in the first place. There were different versions.

After the flood, God had given man the rainbow. It was a gift and a symbol—a promise that this kind of thing would never happen again. Back then there wasn't much in the way of entertainment so when a rainbow came along, it was the closest you got to a drive-in so the tendency was to try to enjoy. But despite its flash, when humans looked upon the rainbow, rather than feeling reassured, they felt a bit like God was trying to dupe them, like he was saying, "Let's forget about all this nasty genocide business and enjoy the pretty colors."

Man did not take God at his word, and it was this lack of trust that Mibzar played on. Mibzar was the youngest son in a family of butchers who worked in Babel.

"I had a dream," Mibzar said to his neighbors. "And in this dream, a new rain came and it made the old rain look like an old lady making pee-pee."

For Mibzar, if it wasn't a prophetic dream, it was headaches, goiters, or excruciating groin pain—anything so long as he had something to yak about, and he was his favorite topic of conversation. Yakking about himself was what came natural to him and he believed it was a talent that would lead him to bigger and better things, better things than simply delivering meat at the butcher shop. And so he stood outside the shop and as people walked by, Mibzar yakked.

"In a dream last night, I saw monkeys underwater," Mibzar cried. "I don't know how much more of this I can take. I have a very sensitive soul. My skin is sensitive, too. I apply ointments of aloe half a dozen times a day and still I have psychosomatic anal welts the size of bees."

He saw that speaking about himself only drew a small crowd, but when he added a twist of flood talk—offered up in high-flown language—more people came to listen and they stayed longer.

"Have you ever seen a tiger underwater? That you should see. Its spine twisting and nails scratching? A tiger, even in his last breath, will try to eat a tuna swimming by because he must obey his calling. But man has a higher calling. Man has things like compassion and kindness. We can only hope that from way up there the Almighty can see that."

Flood debate and speculation was popular in those days. People were still trying to make sense of the whole thing. It was Mibzar's belief that had Noah been more articulate in explaining his conversations with God, he could have made people better understand the consequences of their behavior. And so, Mibzar believed, the flood was largely due to Noah's incompetence as a public speaker.

"I have spoken with God," Mibzar imagined Noah saying, "and He hath commanded me to build an ark. It shall be such and such cubits long, and such and such cubits high and blah blah blah blah."

People were either asleep by the time he was done talking, or back to sodomizing goats and chickens. Mibzar knew that people need a little song and dance. You have to build empathy, otherwise you turn them off.

No, there had to have been a classier way to go about it, a better way to grab people's attention. Mibzar would have included himself in the story—to humanize it. He'd have told them what he ate for breakfast on the day he spoke to God—how the figs he'd consumed were doing a number on his bowels. And most importantly, he would have opened with a joke.

"Do you have any idea what it's like talking to God?" he would have asked in a manner that was warm and conversational. "You think you have a problem speaking in front of a crowd? Try addressing the Creator of the Universe. Build an ark? You got it. Tell me to cut the skin at the fore of my willing-and-able cane and I'll do it!"

It was with his powers as a public speaker at his command that Mibzar undertook what he decided would be his true calling. He would pitch the people of Babel on the idea of building a great monolith. A tower whose top echelons, in the event of another flood, they could flee to. He would oversee its construction and call it "the Tower of Mibzar."

When he first waved over the crowd passing outside the front of his family's butcher shop, Mibzar knew he would need a strong opening line.

"God killed your grandpa," he said. "Don't let him kill your kids. Rainbows and lollipops are one thing, but what I'm proposing is *security*."

"Is that off the rump or a cutlet?" asked a soft-headed roofer named Emile as he peered into the butcher shop.

"This has nothing to do with meat," screamed Mibzar, and one of his brothers came outside and shot him a look that said "Pipe down."

"Look," continued Mibzar, making his voice calm, "I would not even presume to know what the Almighty is thinking. That would be preposterous, but we do have imaginations. It is the way the Fat One in the Sky constructed us, and so we imagine. And I will tell you this: it is my *imagining* that on the day He drowned the whole world, He could not have been feeling very good about himself. It just isn't the behavior of a very self-actualized Almighty. All I'm saying is, who knows what goes through This Guy's head? He's whimsical!"

Mibzar explained his idea for the tower and as he spoke, the crowd around him grew, and as it grew, he became emboldened, explaining it through metaphor, saying it was not so much a prayer to God as it was a prayer to man—a celebration of their humanness. And also their penises.

Along with all of this celebrating, Mibzar offered something else as well: the world's first insurance policy. It would help them sleep better at night. And for Mibzar, it gave him the sense of importance he'd been after his whole life.

*   *   *

The people of Babel were smitten with the idea of a tower and they set to work on it with vigor and purpose. One shift worked all through the morning and another worked through the night. Because of various chronic pains, Mibzar could not actually perform any manual labor, but he stood off to the side for hours, watching the workers as they toiled. When their pace slackened, he threw a few inspirational words their way and, where he saw fit, he peppered his talk with personal anecdotes—about his lifelong battle with foot odor or his childhood fancy for girls with crooked teeth.

On the day he had to stand on his tiptoes to reach the blossoming tower's top, he did a hand-clapping jig that was so pure and unself-conscious that those around him were embarrassed to watch.

"The tower's shade alone will provide a spectacular getaway for a midafternoon siesta," he said, his buttocks gyrating behind him.

In the months that followed, whenever it started to rain, everyone would scramble up the tower laughing like children. Wheee, they'd yell, whizzing up the steps. They knew that whoever got the highest had the best chance of surviving the flood, so there was a fair bit of good-natured jostling.

As the tower grew taller, it could be seen in nearby towns. Curious neighboring villagers came to check it out and once Mibzar explained it all to them in his back-slapping way—making generous mention of his difficult relationship with his father and his problems with mucus in the morning—soon enough, they were immigrating to Babel to work on the tower and take their place in history. And the higher it got, the farther news of the tower spread—and news was spreading far, for now the tower almost poked straight into the clouds.

At night when Mibzar dreamed, it was no longer terrible images of the flood that he saw; it was of himself, ascending the tower. At the very top, he would step onto Heaven's carpet.

"I love what you've done with the place," he'd say to God. Even in dreams, even when standing before the Creator of the Universe, he knew to open with something casual.

The tower slowly grew and as it did, there never seemed any good reason to stop. Everyone was working well together. From Babel and beyond, they all felt like brothers working toward a common goal, and that goal, which had begun as a mere escape ladder, had now become something else—something less easy to define. It had something to do with being more than just a workaday human. It had to do with questing after the infinite. Flood or no flood, they knew their time on Earth would only last so long, and after that—eternal darkness. But with the tower, they'd leave their mark.

As the men worked, Mibzar watched. Making speeches had become exhausting, and so he took to wearing a whistle around his neck, which he blew into to make his wishes known. One toot meant work faster, two toots meant work faster still, and three toots meant send for the lad who scrubs my feet.

Mibzar took to perching himself at the top of the tower and watching the world below. He felt like he could actually *breathe* up there.

"Sometimes it is simpler to gaze upon bald spots than faces," he thought. "Faces always need to be talked to."

Things looked so small down there. The butcher shop, where he had toiled thanklessly for so many years, the site of all his humiliations and petty triumphs—as puny as an ant hill.

"I can crush it with a finger," he said, lifting a pinkie to his eyes.

Mibzar wondered if that was a little how God felt sometimes. Crushy. He wondered, too, if He might like how the tower was bringing the two of them closer together.

He wanted to stay up there all day, in silence, just thinking his thoughts while looking down and allowing his joyous laborers to carry him ever higher, ever closer to God.

But it was on one particularly glorious day of fraternal labor that Mibzar, watching from on high, noticed something was not right. Whereas usually the harmonious sound of men happily working together could be heard—cries of "pass me that bucket of mortar, friend" and "throw me a pickax, my bosom"—now all he could hear were sounds that were garbled, weird, more animal than human. What's more, the jumble sounded panicked—terrified, even.

Mibzar raced down the tower's steps and with his

whistle, summoned one of his foremen. Mibzar looked at him quizzically.

"*Quelque chose de bizarre s'arrive,*" said the foreman.

Annoyed by the man's insubordinate gobbledygook, Mibzar blew his whistle at three men hauling rocks on their backs. The men dropped their loads and trotted over.

"*¿Qué pasa? . . . ¡Qué raro! ¿Qué está saliendo de mi boca?*" said the first man.

"*Hakka Nee-ay shong dong teeyong nee oy eyow,*" said the second.

"*Sento come ho mangiato il fungo magico,*" said the third.

Mibzar tore the whistle from around his neck and spoke.

"*Alk-tay ormal-nay!*"

Upon hearing the strange sounds that escaped his lips, Mibzar covered his mouth as though having emitted a long series of burps. Waiting a few seconds, he tried again.

"*Ut-whay e-thay ell-hay is-way oing-gay on-way?*" he cried. It was as though there was a hand in his mouth, bending and curving his tongue against his will.

For a long while, none of the men dared speak. For Mibzar, it was the first time in his life that his mouth felt like an enemy. The men all stood staring at one another, not knowing what to do. Finally, Mibzar broke the silence. Looking into the heavens, he said in a very quiet voice: *"Od-Gay, ou-yay in-way."*

And as he stared up at the tower, the noonday wind blew through the whistle in his hand in gusts that sounded like high-pitched laughter.

During the days that followed, in the absence of a common language, there was a lot of awkward bowing and smiling—people trying to make themselves understood by talking really loudly and slowly—but it did no good, and after only a week, work on the tower ground to a complete halt. In resigned silence, everyone packed up his tools and journeyed back to his home.

It was hard to return to tending sheep and planting vegetables, though. The work they had done on the tower awakened new hungers in them, hungers they had never known before. They now wanted to create things in the world that were bigger than they were— that would outlast them and instill wonder in the generations to come.

And so they cooked up new ideas. Not high things (they had learned their lesson and wouldn't be opening that can of worms any time soon) but other things. Li wanted to build the world's longest wall; Costa wanted to build a place where hundreds of people could sit in a circle and watch marvelous events; and Bastet, a real cat person, wanted to sculpt the world's biggest feline.

In the months after the men and women of the neighboring towns left, because of how inexperienced they were, most of Babel's tower crumbled away. In the very end, out of the whole thing, only one floor remained—the ground floor—and it was here that Mibzar made his home, opening the world's first language school. Inside, he taught Aramaic as a second language. Mibzar was the kind of teacher who always kept the students way past the end of class, continuing to yak away about himself, or whatever else it was that pleased him.

Jacob and Esau

No matter how many times he heard Rebekah tell the story of the great fight inside her belly, Jacob would get sucked right in. After all, he was its star.

"I think I remember a little," he said. "There was light in there."

"You remember," Rebekah said. "You're such a genius."

His mother was always telling him that. If he drew an X in the sand it was more perfect than God's creation. Made pottage without burning the pan—a hero.

Rebekah would explain, sometimes laughingly and sometimes not, what it felt like to have her belly pulled in opposite directions.

"It was like my lungs were wrestling. From the very beginning you two never got along. My name, Rebekah, means 'she who binds' and how I wished I could bind the two of you to keep you apart. I would rub my stomach to calm you. 'My babies,' I would say. 'What is there to fight for? You are both as close to the one who loves you as can be.' But your brother Esau was never satisfied. He wanted to get in closer. For him, it was not enough to be in me. He wanted to be a part of me. He wanted to swim in my blood like a tuna." She scrunched up her face with distaste and leaned into him.

"Needy," she whispered.

"You were on the left, Jacob. I knew this, and when I stroked you, you became very still. I called you 'Lefty,' which means 'he who is on the left.'

"'Lefty,' I cooed, 'outside in the world I am waiting, my heart bursting with love.' Even then you knew to listen to your mother. Even then we had a special bond. I'll never forget the day you were born."

She never spoke of it as the day *they* were born.

*   *   *

When he thought he was remembering, being in her belly was something like being underwater. Everything was red. It was a whole universe in there, but wherever he swam, there was Esau. Sometimes they bumped heads. Sometimes Esau would grab him and hug him too tightly, making it hard for him to breathe. He sort of recalled he and Esau chewing their mother's bones and trying to stand on each other's shoulders, trying to use the other to get higher. It was a part of some bigger inside joke, but he couldn't quite remember what it was.

"Then I had a dream and in this dream, God spoke to me. And even in the dream I thought, 'How can this be? God doesn't speak to women. Maybe Thou art leaving a message for my husband?' My knees were shaking. 'Wait until your father hears about this,' I thought, because you know about him and God! Isaac's been waiting to hear from Him—has been afraid to hear from Him—since he was a little boy, so a part of me

81

felt bad that I was the one He called out to. But it was funny, too."

Whenever his mother explained this part, she would put the palms of her hands on her thighs. She would imitate the sound of God by making her voice stern and serious, like a nursery teacher's.

"So he says to me, he says, 'Your sons will each father a nation and these nations will not like each other, at all, at all.'"

She threw her hands up in the air as though to say this was all beyond the intellect of a simple shepherd's wife.

"The old women told me that I had a couple of kickers and kickers were healthy. 'But,' I told the old women, 'what I have is more than kickers. They're trying to kill each other!' I feared for your lives and for my own. When I tried to stand still you both knocked me from one end of the house to the other. One night I dreamed that you were both at it again. In the dream I stuck my finger into my belly button to try and separate you, and someone in there tried to pull me in. I woke up screaming. I had begun to give birth."

* * *

"We named Esau Esau, which means 'he who is hairy.' When he was born he looked like a wet little monkey— or one of your father's hairy fists! He was cute," she allowed, "but you! Jacob, you were the light of my life. When your father put you on my belly I just laughed and laughed and cried and laughed and cried some more. My cheeks were raw from where the old women slapped to calm me down. One hundred, two hundred slaps and still I laughed and cried. I was out of my mind with ecstasy. Making you was the best thing I ever did."

"And Esau, too?" Jacob asked.

"I love *all* of my children," she said soberly.

The way Jacob heard it, he had been born with his hand gripped on to Esau's foot. It was like he was holding on to the string of a balloon that was slowly rising out of the red universe.

In those days being the oldest was serious business, and since Esau came out first, everything was to go to him. The birthright, the Big Blessing. Everything.

As children, Esau would always make sure to introduce Jacob as his baby brother.

"How can you call me that?" Jacob would ask. "I came out five minutes after you. Five lousy minutes!"

"And so I will always be five minutes ahead of you. Five minutes wiser. Five minutes more seasoned. Doesn't it make you feel safe? Like you have a battering ram pushing on ahead of you into the future? I would tell you what it's like here in the future, but you know I'm not very good with words."

Esau acted like it was a photo finish at the derby. There he was at the finish line, carrying flowers and posing for portraits, Jacob's hand still clamped desperately on to his foot.

Isaac, Rebekah, Jacob, and Esau would all lie in bed. They were a bed family. With Isaac lying down all day, it was the only way they could all spend time together.

Jacob and Esau would rub Rebekah's back.

"See if you can tell if it's me or Jacob," said Esau and, every time, Rebekah was able to tell.

"Your touch restores me," she would tell Jacob afterward. "I don't know why. You're so good, Jacob. Please don't be mad. I know you love your brother."

When Esau was alone, he would sometimes pack things up his nose—barley, grass, pebbles. It was his hobby and Rebekah found it gross. She would turn away and gag, or pretend to gag. Isaac said packing things up or picking things out of the nose were signs of a deep thinker. But one day Esau packed too much sponge up there and couldn't get it out. Isaac had to pull back the tip of his nose to get a look. He held Esau in his arms as he screamed and pleaded.

"It'll be okay," Isaac said. There were tears in his eyes.

Rebekah and Jacob turned away. Rebekah started to laugh, just a little, and then so did Jacob. It was just too ridiculous.

Afterward, Esau spent the day breathing really loudly through his nose, like breathing through wide-open nostrils was a treat—a gift from God. The sound drove Jacob crazy.

"Let me tell you a secret," his mother would say. Jacob would go over and sit in her lap. She would whisper in his ear: "It is you I love best."

He would look at his mother and it was like looking into the void. It was from where he sprang and sometimes it felt unnatural to be so close to the source of his own existence. Sometimes he couldn't understand why he didn't run as far away as he could—just leap from the dinner table in midbite and run. To stick around and chat with the person that encircles the hole from which you crept out of the infinite was just sort of—awkward.

But his mother loved him so much. She told him that Esau had come out first for no reason and that she didn't want the big dumb universe making important decisions for her and him.

"But maybe it was God's decision for Esau to come out first," Jacob said.

Rebekah scrunched up her face.

"Please," she said.

When they were kids, Esau liked pretending. He talked in high-pitched voices and walked all over on his all-fours like a cat.

There is no sadder word than "family," thought Jacob.

For Esau, Jacob's heart was always just about to break. He imagined little cracks in it, the guilt leaking out like gray egg yolk flowing through the pristine white tubes inside him.

"You did this to me," he imagined screaming at Rebekah. "Everything."

Jacob had this memory of every single child in the neighborhood chasing Esau down the street. They threw rocks and brandished sticks. How is such a thing even possible? They were only four. How could they organize themselves into an angry mob, and why would they?

But Jacob remembered being with them, telling them all the things that only a brother could know. "Esau cries like a baby when I sing certain songs. Esau smells his own toes. Esau lies on his stomach and pulls his ass cheeks apart and laughs."

"Esau. Esau," the crowd chanted and Jacob was among them. Esau ran through the streets weeping, a mustache of mucus. It was like he was being chased back into nonexistence.

*   *   *

"You're the Cain," Jacob said when they were playing alone. It just popped into his head—a genius thought.

"You're the Cain," Esau answered uncertainly. No one had taught Esau how to believe in himself, how to fight.

"No. You're the Cain." Jacob said it with so much calm certainty that Esau just gave up. Every mother has one Cain and one Abel. That's just how it goes. Jacob knew this.

During his adolescence, Esau went through this period where he decided that Rebekah would love him more if he wasn't so hairy. So he cut and pulled the hair from his body.

Jacob walked in on him. Esau stood naked and shaking, fistfuls of hair clutched in his hands.

"The air feels so weird on my skin," he said. There were patches of white flesh polka-dotting his body.

It got so bad that Isaac had to talk to him.

"Look at me," Isaac said. "Being hairy hasn't kept me from achieving any of my goals."

Esau had no idea what any of his father's goals were. Wandering the forest? Lying in bed? Still, he appreciated his father's effort.

"Look," said Isaac, putting his hairy forearm against Esau's hairy forearm. "The same."

As Esau got older, he grew into his hairiness. He became large and outdoorsy. He even began to like the way he looked a little. He said body hair was practical, that he could feel bugs crawling on him and swat them before they could bite. He made jokes about Jacob's smoothness and Jacob defended himself by saying he was more streamlined—that it helped him run faster.

"If you oiled yourself up, sanded your nipples down, and tucked your serpent between your legs, I could shoot you into the sky like an arrow!" laughed Esau. When Esau laughed his face just froze, his eyes half open.

He was having fun and wanted to keep the good times rolling.

"You know how Mom gets that weird thing when you're out with her at the market where she insists on having you call her by her name? 'Stop calling me *Mom*,' she says. 'My name is Rebekah.' What's that all about? She trying to pick up men?"

Esau's laughter started in his loins and blasted out through his nostrils. His mouth, open wide. His head tilted to the side. His eyes not laughing.

"Lighten up and have a good time," Esau said when he saw Jacob silently studying him.

"By your telling me to have a good time—it doesn't *make* me have a good time. In fact, it only makes me have less of a good time."

Esau was always trying to be a party animal. It was painful to watch. He would put his arm around a stranger's neck and bob his head up and down to some song only he could hear, one of his hands holding on to a chicken leg and the other a beer. This was not joie de vivre. This was something else, something that made Jacob's stomach ache.

"Whoo," Esau would say. "Ha ha."

Jacob looked at him, his brother's sadness sweating out of his pores, stinking up the night.

* * *

"You were so easy," she said. "Never a problem. Never a day of heartache. I could have had a hundred of you."

He tried to imagine it. A hundred Jacobs, all trying to fit into the bathtub at the same time. All smiling painfully, his mother scrambling from Jacob to Jacob, whispering in each of their ears.

"I love you more than any other Jacob," she'd say to each one as she made her rounds.

A hundred Jacobs unable to look each other in the eye. A hundred Jacobs sighing so loudly, in unison, that it would shake the heavens like a lion's roar.

He wanted to sway her. He thought about some of the things that made Esau likable. He couldn't think well under pressure.

"You should just let him know you like him. Because I know you do."

"Oh, Jacob," she said. "You're so compassionate. I could have had a *thousand* of you."

* * *

"He'll waste his birthright," she said. "He's so stupid."

She scrunched up her face.

"You'd be doing him a favor," she said.

Esau came in from hunting, dragging behind him carcasses, beaks, and tusks. It left a trail of greasy blood and made the house smell like sweaty back hair and death.

Jacob was by the stove mixing a small pot. He was wearing Rebekah's apron.

"I swear to God when I walked in here and saw you in that thing I thought you were Mom," said Esau.

"It keeps my clothes clean," said Jacob, stirring and bristling.

"Whatever you say, m'lady. Pass me a little pottage. I'm about to drop dead from hunger."

Jacob thought for a moment.

"I'll give you a big heaping bowl," said Jacob, "but there's a little something I'd like from you in return."

"A pair of oven mitts to go with your apron?" asked

Esau, letting loose what he believed to be the good hardy laugh of a man who'd been hunting all day. "I'll tell you what: In my pockets I've got a couple hedgehogs I've slaughtered. You can stick your pudgy little ball-handlers in each of their arses."

Esau's laughter filled the room. Goosing Jacob, wrapping its hairy arms around him, sticking its fingers into his heart and trying to pry stuff out.

"I want your birthright," said Jacob.

"The parchment?" For that was what Esau called it. Jacob had seen it around—lying among Esau's underwear.

"What do you want with that old thing?" asked Esau. "God knows where I even put it."

"Find it and I will feed you."

"Everything's a hustle with you," said Esau. "Here I am, starving to death, and you're working an angle."

Esau tramped off to find the crumpled little ball. Years later, when Jacob recalled the transaction, he would see in his mind how *fast* Esau had tramped off. As eager as his brother was to eat that day, he was even more eager to simply be liked.

* * *

"You know," said Esau, shoveling back the stew, "how Mom gets that look when she looks at you? How she wrinkles up her face like she's just smelled spoiled goat milk? She was just doing it to me this morning. I was telling her about my plans for the summer, about the summer hut I want to build, and she was doing the face. Do it for me. You do the best Mom."

When they were kids it was one of the only jokes they shared. Jacob imitating their mother.

"You throw your shekels away on nonsense," Jacob would say, his hands on his hips. It didn't take much to get his brother rolling around on the floor.

"Just do Mom," Esau begged. "With the apron on it'll be perfect."

"You talk too much about Mom," Jacob said.

Jacob felt sorry for Rebekah. He knew Isaac couldn't have been an easy man to live with. He was always off to himself, removed. Ruminating. Wandering the woods. Considering climbing a tree. Deciding not to.

"You don't come within two seconds of having your father murder you and have your life end up a big party," said Rebekah. "That little boy was broken that day."

Rebekah said that when she was young she was a good dancer, but Isaac never wanted to dance with her.

"He's too heavy to dance," she said.

At parties she would dance while Isaac sat watching from his chair. She would wave to him. He would smile and wave back.

"As he's gotten older, all he does is wait around to hear from God all day and he's afraid it could happen any moment so he doesn't want to be doing something undignified when it does. He's in and out of the bathroom in five seconds flat and he's careful never to get food in his beard."

Then she stopped, leaned forward, started, licked her lips, stopped, leaned back, and started again.

"Don't ever get married," she said, her eyes full of love.

When Jacob heard the story, it was never from Isaac. It was usually from old friends of the family, sometimes from Rebekah. He always wanted more details. He wanted to know if Grandpa Abraham had said any-thing to Isaac first. "No hard feelings," or something to explain that he had no choice—that he was just follow-ing orders. He wondered if they had walked back home together afterward and what they might have talked about along the way.

He wondered if Isaac had ever said to himself, "I'm never going to do stuff like that to my kid. Me, I'm just going to lie in bed all day. Wander the woods. Keep to myself. Stay out of trouble."

Jacob was glad God never bothered trying to get in touch with him. It was always bad news with That Guy.

As Isaac's health got worse, he started to disappear into himself. He'd lie on his side in bed, the sheets drawn up past his chin. Rebekah said he was afraid of the angels. He saw tiny ones all over the walls. They were like moths, but with faces. His eyesight was failing him, and aside from the angels he could hardly see a thing.

"Now is the time," Rebekah said. "He hasn't much longer to live. I've sent Esau out to hunt for him. Go to your father now."

She had been bugging Jacob with her plan for weeks. Esau was supposed to get Isaac's Big Blessing, the one given from the deathbed that goes to the firstborn. But Rebekah had other plans. She thought that if Jacob dressed up in Esau's clothes he could get the blessing instead of Esau.

"Let him have the blessing," said Jacob, waving her off. "He needs it more than I do."

"Believe me," she said, "you'd be doing him a favor."

"How would stealing our father's final blessing be doing him a favor?"

She waved her hand dismissively.

"He'd waste it on whores."

Jacob tried to talk her out of it. He tried to talk himself out of it.

"But if he touched me," he said, "he'd know I'm not Esau."

"Please," she said. "We'll stick some goatskin to your arms and neck and stink you up a bit. You'll be fine."

Jacob wondered: if you tricked a blessing out of someone, did it devalue it? Inverse it? After all, the universe's workings have always been more than somewhat ironic.

* * *

It smelled like eucalyptus and sweat. Out of the dark all he could hear was "Esau. Esau."

Jacob timidly walked toward his father's bed. He feared that Isaac, so close to Heaven, could sense his fear the way animals could. He tried to relax himself. "This wasn't your idea," he repeated to himself. Somehow this notion soothed him. He was just doing it for her. He was being a good son. He pretended he had no will, that he was a golem—a blessing-stealing golem brought to life through the force of his mother's will, through incantations whispered in his ear.

Still, the thoughts came: *This is the worst thing anyone has ever done to anyone in the history of all creation. Even when Cain killed Abel it was probably a crime of passion. Who goes on to bigger and better things after a stunt like this?* He moved closer. He stood over Isaac's bed.

"Sit," his father said.

They sat, not saying anything, Isaac's heavy breathing filling the room. The goatskin was scratchy against Jacob's skin.

His father stared at him with wild eyes that really looked like they could see.

"My son, my seed, my life, my joy," said Isaac, and then Jacob just zoned out. He stared into his father's eyes and blocked out the sound of the world. Maybe Isaac was blessing Esau anyhow. Maybe it didn't matter that he was holding his hand.

When he was done, Isaac kept raising his forearm to him and smiling.

"The same," he said.

Jacob had no idea what the gesture or the words were supposed to mean. He grabbed his father's forearm with his hand and, making his voice as gravelly and out-doorsy as possible, told his father to rest.

When Esau got home from the hunt he saw Jacob in his shawl of goatskin. He started to laugh, but then he understood and his laughter stopped. It frightened Ja-cob how quickly his brother understood. He began to talk and Esau ran past him.

"Let him," Rebekah said.

Esau went to Isaac's room. Then Isaac understood. He still wanted Esau to have a blessing, too, but his strength was diminishing and his blessing-power was weak. After the passion of the Big Blessing with Jacob, he was burned out.

Still, he took Esau to his side and gave him what he had left.

"Bless thee. Bless thee. May thine health be passable and thine income middling. May thou find a bride of so-so looks and mediocre bust. May thine days pass with relative tolerableness." And so it went.

Rebekah saw the look in Esau's eyes and knew he would be out for blood. She told Jacob that he must flee.

Jacob was nauseous. He was not the fleeing kind. He told her he wanted to try to talk to Esau, but Rebekah said it was past all that.

"Now there is only running," she said. "You know how he gets."

Rebekah had a brother in Haran named Laban. She told Jacob to go to him.

"He'll take care of you," she said. "He's just like you. You're both my favorites."

"What about your husband? And Esau?" Jacob asked. He didn't know why he even bothered.

"I love them, too," she said evenly. "I just have a very special place in my heart for you and Laban."

Apparently Laban was the other light of his mother's life—a demigod who could do no wrong. Jacob hardly remembered him. They had only met once, years ago, when Jacob was a small child. He had been building a tower of blocks when Laban walked in and kicked it over.

"Make no Babels," he said.

"Laban, you're wicked," his mother laughed.

Jacob stood at the edge of the field with Rebekah.

"Do you remember when I was a child and you told me that you liked me better than Esau? Why did you do that?"

"Because it was true."

"But why did you think I needed to know this? Did you think it would make me happy?"

"I guess I wasn't a very good mother," she said, her hands twisting up.

"You were a very good mother," he said, backing off.

"I couldn't help it. I tried my best."

"I know."

"It was different back then. I see how modern mothers are now. I didn't know any better."

Jacob sat in silence, thinking about his brother. Before he left, his mother hugged him tightly. She looked at his face.

"I love you more than life itself," she said.

"Ma, please. Why do you have to tell me these things?"

"I just want you to be happy," she wept, her whole body shaking.

After Jacob moved away, Esau took care of Rebekah but still, she wouldn't give in, wouldn't give him her full love the way she did with Jacob. Esau knew it and she knew he knew it. It was a thing they shared. She held on to her love as though holding on to it was a mark of character, as though love was gold that you had to be thrifty with. And so every second she spent with Esau, it was like there was some part of her, deep down, that was shaking its head and saying, over and over, "Nope."

Still, Esau couldn't help but try. He even put her whole role in the blessing thing out of his mind. He put all of his hate on Jacob and in this way, Jacob got a double share.

Rebekah talked about Jacob all the time and Esau let her. He even made an effort to keep the conversation going. If he had anything Jacob-related to say, he was guaranteed his mother's full attention.

"I will concede that he had an above average singing voice," said Esau, "but he did *not* have blond hair. Light brown at best. Blond it was not."

And the whole time, Esau knew that Jacob was out there.

"Gamboling, sashaying, waving the parchment—bathed in the ever-blondening halo of our father's sweet deathbed blessing."

Then came the pain. It started in the balls and twisted its way into his stomach. On some days it was so bad that he'd get afraid he'd have to spend the rest of his life walking around doubled over, holding on to his groin. God forbid he should become one of those guys! He was not even sure if there *were* such guys. He would be the first.

Not only had Jacob destroyed his life but his memory continued to destroy it a little more every day—breaking off a new piece of his soul here and there. That was the true miracle of life: whenever you thought you'd been completely crushed, there was always a little something left to get creamed.

It was one day while sitting on a log, indulging his new hobby of twisting his beard until the pain became unbearable, that Esau met a girl from Canaan named Linda. She was into the dark, brooding type and soon she and Esau began dating. Linda was a good companion and she took Esau's mind off his troubles.

After seeing Linda for some time, Esau finally presented his mother with the burning question.

"Do you like her?" he asked.

"I like her if you like her," she said, never looking up from her chicken plucking.

Linda came from a family of idol worshippers. Rebekah referred to her as "the Little Idol Worshipper Girl."

"There's more to her than idol worship," Esau said. He tried to come up with one or two things—how she was really nice to him, how she loved him—but he knew his mother would find all of that stuff corny.

*   *   *

Meanwhile in Haran, Jacob's life was no bed of roses either. His uncle Laban worked him like a red-maned pack mule. And after he fell in love with Laban's youngest daughter, Rachel—that was when his troubles really began. It was then that he stupidly, drunkenly—blue-balledly—agreed to work for seven years in Laban's service in exchange for her hand in marriage.

The next day, waking up flaccid, he tried to renegotiate the deal.

"Seven years?" he asked incredulously. "It doesn't strike you as excessive?"

"Afraid of the smell of your own work sweat?" asked Laban. "Rebekah always said you were a pussy."

Jacob had never loved anyone like he loved Rachel. Sometimes it was a nice feeling, but often it terrified him. She felt more real than anything in the world, even himself. Sometimes he would get so insecure, he'd ask her ten times in a day, "You still love me, right?"

"No, I hate you," she'd say, smiling. She was so young and didn't know her strength. It scared Jacob to death. He felt like his life was not his own. His life felt like it was being batted around by a baby. At night he dreamed she was a kitten that he chased through holes and under the ground, crying. It was like there was always the risk of her wandering off, his heart in her teeth. In this way, Jacob was made humble by coming to know what pain really was. He wanted to marry Rachel even if it meant nothing *but* pain. He would sit on a chair made of cactus needles for the rest of his life if only to have her with him, seated upon his lap.

So for seven years, Jacob tended flocks and raised cattle and finally, at the end of the term, his bride was presented to him. But after the marriage ceremony, when Jacob lifted the bridal veil, he discovered not Rachel, but her older sister, Leah.

Jacob was furious. When he asked Laban what was going on, all he got was a shit-eating grin.

"Let's not get hung up with details on such a day of rejoicing." Then, closing the book on the whole thing, he scrunched up his face.

Jacob didn't push it. In a weird way he felt he had it coming, having been a proponent of the old switcheroo

106

himself. There were Leah's feelings to consider, too. She felt so low.

"My father," she had wept in explanation.

So Jacob just married Rachel as well. Then he had two wives. Just thinking about the cousins that would be brothers and the daughters who would be nieces was enough to give him a headache. But at least he had Rachel.

It was around this time that Jacob heard the voice of God. He heard it in a dream and, oddly, the voice took the form of Rebekah's imitation of the voice of God.

"Mom?" asked Jacob, "is that you?" His mother had been dead several years.

"It is God!" spoke Rebekah's voice. "If thou heard my actual voice even for half a second thou would instantly go mad and then be of no use to anyone. Maybe some day thou might be ready for it, but not now."

The voice commanded him to go back to Canaan. But Esau was in Canaan. What would going back home accomplish?

"My brother will only kill me there," said Jacob. "Thou *knowest* how he gets."

"Go and I shall watch over you."

So Jacob packed up the family and went back to Canaan.

When he got to the outskirts of town, Jacob sent a messenger to seek out his brother.

"Wha'd he say?" asked Jacob when the messenger returned.

"He shall come with an army of four hundred."

"Did he actually say army? He didn't say welcoming committee, or coterie? Chefs? Musicians? Tell me exactly what he said—to the word."

"'I shall come with an army of four hundred.'"

"Where does he get a figure like that? Doesn't that seem a little excessive?"

Later that night, unable to sleep, Jacob tried to do the arithmetic: Five men to torture each finger and nail. Five per toe. One to rip open each nostril and one to stick fire in. Three to pull head hair and three to do beard hair. Two to eye-gouge, two to ear-stab, ten to back-pound. Fourteen for charley horses. And ten of the more eloquent men to admonish him for being such a bad brother. That still left over two hundred men with nothing to do but stand around drawing a salary. His brother had always been prone to high-rolling and flash.

Still sleepless, he went over his calculations again. This time, including torture of the joints and flaying of the skin, he accounted for three hundred and nine men. When he opened his eyes Jacob saw he was not alone, for squatting beside him was an angel.

The angel smiled beatifically. Then, drawing his wings back like the ears of an angry cat, he dropped his elbow onto Jacob's groin. After that it was all nonstop pile drivers and headlocks.

All of Esau's murderous rage and hatred had come to life in the form of a heavenly wrestling angel! Or maybe he'd decided to just hire the angel instead of the army. Either way, Jacob was getting his ass handed to him. Hiding beside a rock in the darkness, he caught his breath. Once it was caught, he ran toward the angel, screaming and crying, his arms doing a Dutch windmill. The angel caught him by the throat and bear-hugged him. His flesh was cool and Jacob noted his breath smelled of daffodils. He wondered: *In Heaven, do they eat flowers?* Breaking free of the angel's hold, he reared back his fist and punched him in the nose. *Maybe his dad was the one who saved my dad's life.* The angel flew into the sky and immediately Jacob felt ashamed. *What kind of a person punches an angel in the face?* He had never even heard of anyone *touching* an angel. He looked at the angel blood on his fist—red, almost purple—and felt like a sleazebag, but not for long, as the angel flew back down, stomping his foot onto the top of Jacob's skull.

And so it went. Throughout the night, they wrestled like a couple of schoolyard kids. As the hours went by, Jacob tried anything to get the angel to leave him be— tickling him, screaming in his face, biting his wings— but there was no stopping him. Sometimes Jacob would start to laugh, thinking, *This is the stupidest thing I've ever done in my life,* but then he was right back to inverted face-locking, camel-clutching, and mandible-clawing.

When the morning came, the angel had to get back to Heaven, but Jacob wouldn't let him leave. He felt that he had gone too far to just back off. He gripped on to the angel's foot.

"Bless me," demanded Jacob.

Still smiling, the angel punched him on the Adam's apple.

"How many blessings does one person need?" asked the angel. "Do not be a blessing hog at the Lord's trough."

Still, Jacob would not let go of his foot. He wanted to at least get one normal thing out of the whole experience, something that wasn't embarrassing to tell people about.

The angel flapped his wings and kicked his legs but Jacob's grip held firm.

"All right. I bless thee. Thy new blessed name is Israel."

Jacob released the angel's foot and watched him flap away into the sky. He wanted nothing more than to get some sleep, but there was no time. *Israel* had to meet his brother.

Jacob had his people send forth to his brother a gift.

"Make it munificent," said Jacob, and his people sent out camels, cattle, and sheep. Esau, as it turned out, was very warmed by the gesture and when the brothers met, Esau bowed and Jacob bowed back. There followed a great deal of bowing. It started off sheepishly and slowly but became more and more heartfelt. In the end the two brothers were practically belly flopping at each other's feet. All the while, Esau's army stood around them in a huge circle. Jacob could not help thinking of the money their just standing there and not painfully killing him was wasting.

Finally, Esau spoke.

"I received your gifts," he said. "They were really munificent."

Esau introduced his brother to each of the four hundred men in his army. Jacob gave up trying to remember their names after the fourth one.

"Everything I told you about this guy," said Esau, his hand on his brother's shoulder, "forget it."

"There's one more thing I have for you."

Jacob handed Esau the flattened-out piece of parchment.

"It's really yours," he said.

Esau protested but Jacob, who was still all wrestly from his match with the angel, started to get physical about it—awkwardly shoving it down his brother's toga.

Later in the evening, once they had begun to loosen

up, a spread of food was prepared. As they ate, and
Esau got into the warmth and spirit, without thinking,
and under Jacob's stunned gaze, he pulled out the rum-
pled parchment and used it to wipe a spot of gravy from
off his chin.

"Dad would be so happy to see us like this," said Jacob.

"For a long time, all I wanted to do was murder you,"
said Esau. "On some days it was the only thing that
kept me going." He motioned a chicken leg toward the
army. They were playing dice and drinking merrily.

"I wanted to kill you well—everything just so. Now
I have four hundred men to feed. For what?"

Jacob smiled.

"You've changed," he said. "Your shoulder hair is
practically white." He stopped, not wanting to disre-
spect him. "Like snowcapped mountains, I mean."

Esau laughed.

"You seem different, too."

The angel's thigh punches had given Jacob a slight
limp. It helped him to come off as less of a hotshot.

Jacob told him about how he had fallen in love and

how it made him see life differently. From love he quickly wound his way toward the subject of his father-in-law. Once he got going, Rachel joined in with extra details about her father's douchery—just to keep the party vibe going.

Esau listened with a serious look on his face. He liked the way life was now able to get his brother worked up.

"I wrestled an angel last night," said Jacob, happily jumping from subject to subject. They were learning to converse. It was like learning to walk—together, bound to one another under one toga.

"You know," said Rachel, "it's crazy how much you look alike."

The twins looked at each other silently, their faces relaxed. It was like gazing into a clear pond on a summer day.

"Sometimes I wake up screaming at her," Esau said. "My wife tells me I'm crazy."

But then their conversation turned to other things, cattle and the weather, and they did not talk of Rebekah. They did not speak of the hand that had wiped away their tears, how now it was bereft of flesh, how now it wore a bracelet made of worms. It would have done no good to have spoken of any of it.

The Golden Calf

After forty intense days with God, Moses descended Mount Sinai, his nerves shot. No sooner had he reached the base of the mountain than he heard music coming from a nearby clearing. Looking through the trees, he saw the children of Israel praying to what appeared to be a crudely sculpted golden calf. They danced and pranced—flounced, frisked, strutted, and swaggered. All hopped up on idol worship.

Cranky by disposition but made even more irritable by lack of sleep, Moses began to weep tears of anger. Even the people he'd trusted—the wise, loyal ones—tapping their feet and snapping their fingers like it was a hootenanny!

Golden calves were all the rage, but Moses had warned them before he left. "I'll be down in a jiff," he had said, "so don't start praying until I get back."

Seeing their lurid dance, Moses took the tablets he was carrying—tablets bearing commandments he had transcribed for *them*—commandments that, among other things, commanded there be no other god but God—God god—and he dropped them to the ground. Though Moses could get angrier than just about anyone besides God, he dropped them not in his wrath. For Moses this was odd, as he ate, spoke, slept, and snored in his wrath. He could even whistle a tune in his wrath! But when he let the tablets fall to the earth, he did it like an overburdened little kid who just didn't care anymore. That was when Moses was at his scariest: when he was all quiet and holding back.

The children of Israel stared at him in silent terror.

"Zero commandments for you," he repeated quietly under his breath.

*   *   *

You would think that that would spell the end for golden calves, but this was not the case. There was still one man holding out hope, a man who thought monotheism just another fad. This man's name was Gomer and he was the largest golden calf dealer in the Sinai region and, much to his son Ian's embarrassment, he had a real "never say die" attitude.

"They'll come around," Gomer said to his son soon after the commandment episode. "An invisible God that no one can see except Moses? Oh, and He's also got a temper problem—likes to make threats and burn bushes. I don't want to pray like a frightened mouse. I want to pray as one equal to another. And those laws—'Don't wear this cloth with that cloth! Don't let this cattle graze with that cattle!' All that red tape. Not for me."

But the god of Moses did make a splash with a great many people. When Moses got going, waving his staff around while yelling bloody murder—curing leprosy and transforming his rod into a snake—he made a pretty persuasive case. People became fired up on New God and began forming mobs of protest in front of Gomer's showroom. But still, Gomer was undeterred.

"Business is business," he said to his son as they

watched the crowd grow, through a crack in the door. "Is there a commandment that says 'Thou shalt regulate trade'? No way. Remember when they said candied manna was sacrilege? I rode it out and two weeks later I was selling it on a stick!"

It was true Ian's father was an innovator. When he got into the business it was all cows, full grown, but Gomer saw that as homes got smaller there was a need for an idol that could fit more neatly into a corner— something you could drape a caftan over and prop your feet on when you weren't worshipping. And thus the mini cow, or "calf," was born.

"What makes the god of Moses better than my calves?" Gomer asked. "What can he do that they can't? Speak in that sonorous voice that makes you feel like you just swallowed your balls? Bullshit. That's not being a god. That's just being pushy. The Calf is a more laid back, cud-chewing lord. He minds his own business and only steps in in a pinch. Remember when I prayed for the bastard selling silver goats next door to get dropsy? And did he not deliver? All praise the Golden Bovine, whose gold trumps silver, whose golden teats nourish us with invisible golden milk."

Gomer stopped his pantomime of teat-squeezing and

looked at his son to see if he was making an impression. He was not.

"You heard Moses talk on the mountain," Ian said, "the deep grumbly voice—the water into blood. It gave everyone the same feeling. We all said so: The tingling in the chest. The rattling of the rib cage. You said you felt it, too."

"You know me," Gomer said. "I don't want to hurt feelings. If someone gets excited I get excited, too. But someone does a few magic tricks and you renounce everything you ever stood for? I was born a Golden Calf man and I shall die a Golden Calf man. Integrity. It's the way my daddy raised me and, if I'm not mistaken, it's how I raised you."

Gomer had raised him to be cheap, suspicious, and sneaky. He didn't know where integrity fit in.

"They'll come around," Gomer said. But as the days went by and the angry crowd outside his showroom grew in number, Gomer saw that people weren't coming around.

"What we need is a battle plan," he said.

And so Gomer invited over his brothers. A bigger bunch of shysters, hoodwinkers, and chicanerous pettifoggers there never was. Ian hated when they all got together. In five minutes the whole house smelled of farts and his cheeks were pinched black and blue.

Brother number one sold discount winnowing shovels that broke the second you winnowed; brother number two was a professional angel spotter ("There's one right behind you!" he'd cry. "You just missed him!"); and brother number three was a bookie who took bets on the weather. Every time Ian saw him he'd grab him by the sleeve and try to explain something called the "Sunny Day Trifecta."

"Three rainy days in a row, or you box it with one sunny day and two rainy. Then you get some rotten s.o.b. telling you he felt drops! But drops ain't rain!"

Ian, wanting to avoid the ordeal of their visit, offered to voyage out to the Wilderness of Sin to purchase dried fruit, but Gomer told him to stay put.

"I have a warehouse full of the golden fuckers," said Gomer, for this was the way they talked when they were all together. It was fucker this and fucking fuckballs that.

"We have to tactically leverage this fuck," said brother number one.

"We have to rebrand the fuck-face," added brother number two.

When all together, they became one big fat "we." Ian would try to get into the spirit of it and "we" along with them, but his "we's" always got caught in his throat.

"The name 'Golden Calf' scares people," said brother number three gravely. "We could start calling them 'Festive Cows.'"

"But 'Golden Calf' is a name the public knows," Gomer reminded them.

"We have to distance ourselves from all that. We can sell cow clothes. Dress 'em up in the latest styles. Tunics! Prayer shawls! Princess Golden Cow for girls. Slap a beard on the fuck-ass and you've got a Moses Cow. We'll call him 'Mooses.' A beautiful tribute! We can accessorize. Golden tablets! A golden walking staff!"

"It's still a golden calf," said Ian. "It's just different names for what it is: an idol."

"Just a different name! Look at the weeping willow. Would you seek its shade were it an overflowing shit bucket bush?"

Then Ian felt his cheek clamped, twisted, pulled, and finally snapped back into place.

"Jackass," his uncle said with affection.

If the brothers had lived in Egypt during the ten plagues and had owned a boat shack, they'd have gone out in the streets, pitching, the very night the rivers turned to blood.

"But have you *tasted* the waters?" they'd exclaim, licking their chops. "My hand to Rah—cherry borscht!"

They'd have seen each of the nine ensuing plagues as nine distinct business opportunities. Cursed darkness? Let's-make-babies night! Hail mixed with fire? Refreshing joy nuggets and fun-time ouchie bolts!

"Can't we just melt them down and get into a new business?" asked Ian.

"What kind of new business?" brother number one asked, pinching his cheek with warmth.

"Something a little less . . . contentious," said Ian.

Gomer and his brothers decided that melting down the idols was not an option since half their value was in the craftsmanship. For the brothers the case was closed, but Ian still worried. When he'd go outside to try to calm the agitated crowd, he'd end up learning a lot about New God. His résumé was impressive: divided the Heavens from the Earth, made man from the dust, created the universe—the list went on and on.

When Ian walked outside, the mob swarmed him. The questions were always the same.

"What can your god do?" the crowd demanded.

Never any good under the gun, Ian stuttered and back-pedaled.

"You can polish him," he said, "and lean against him, too."

"The Golden Calf is strictly local," said an intense and scholarly-looking young man named Rodney. "Ram-headed Sun gods. Hawk-bodied Earth gods—it's so childish."

"But your god . . . God?"

"You mustn't even speak His actual name!" interrupted Rodney. "He doesn't like it, so we've invented nick-names for Him: He Who Will Kill You. He Who Will Crush You. He Who Will Set You On Fire and Douse the Flames with the Blood of Those You Love. You really have to be careful. The Beneficent One hears all and sees all."

Ian began to feel New God's gaze upon him all the time now. Especially when he was voiding his bowels. He was scared of this new god and sometimes even believed he could smell Him. When there was burning in the air, he pictured the angry smoke escaping New God's ears.

"The consummate god is a forgiving god," they said on the street. Still, he was scared. For himself and for his father.

And then the rioting began. "No more idols!" they chanted. "Our god trumps all gods."

Gomer remained unimpressed. He felt protected by the Calf.

"For such a powerful god," he said, "Invisible God is surprisingly thin-skinned."

"Ours is a jealous god," said Ian.

Gomer was struck silent by his son's words. He stared at Ian a good long time. As a rule, Gomer was never nonplussed. But his son's words—they nonplussed him.

"I see," Gomer said, nervously massaging coins through the thin leather of his money pouch. "So now he's *your* god."

"There's no choice," Ian said. "He's taking over."

"But what about graven images?" asked Gomer. "With your new god there will be none of that! And you love a good graven image! I don't get it. When you were little, you adored the god of your father." Gomer reached over and pinched his son's cheeks with sadness. "What happened?"

"He's omnipotent," said Ian, using a word he'd just learned from Rodney. "He can outfight, outthink, and outrace any god you throw at Him."

"I'll get my brothers in here and we'll cook up a new god. We'll call him 'Omnipotent Plus One'!"

"This is embarrassing," Ian said. "It's also dangerous."

"I didn't realize I was embarrassing you," Gomer said, his pinching fingers limp.

That night, Gomer remained in the showroom, pacing from calf to calf, ruminating.

"What is there for a father to pass down to a son if not his god?" Gomer wondered.

He did not like this new god. He was uncanny, grandiose, and bloodthirsty, but Gomer could also sense that he might have staying power. Even Rah couldn't work a crowd like This Guy.

And so, the very next day, he brought in the alchemists with their enormous black cauldrons. He knew it would likely mean taking a tremendous beating on the value and he knew it would mean having to shout his brothers down, but Gomer vowed that every last golden hock and udder would be melted. His new idea was to remold the gold into long, thin wands with pointing little index fingers at the tip.

"We'll market them as commandment pointers," said Gomer, "to help you read the word of God. You know . . . God god."

The brothers mulled it over. After a long silence, they spoke.

"Give the people what they want," said brother number one, who knew when to stand down.

"Gold is gold," said brother number two.

"Yep," said brother number three distractedly, for in his mind he was already on to a dozen other hog swindles.

Ian watched the calves melt, their little calf faces poking out of the pots, looking at him. They made him feel almost as guilty as the sight of his father's face, which was wet and glowing in the heat of the showroom.

When he was a child, Ian could pray so hard. Harder than anyone he knew. It was his thing. He'd squint his eyes, and he'd scrunch up his face. He'd look like he was going to burst a blood vessel, his hands in fists, hoping—willing the world to be a certain way. For the house to quiet down. For good things to happen. For Gomer to notice what a good prayer he was.

When he would finish praying and he'd look around and the world was pretty much the way it had always been, the one thing he felt he could rely on was that the Calf was keeping count, giving out points for effort. At least the Calf knew how hard he was trying.

New God made sense to him, but the Calf made sense to his heart. It was such a part of his childhood— like the smell of certain foods or the tunes his father whistled when they took walks together.

As the years wore on, Ian would often invite Gomer to come and pray with him to New God, and Gomer would tag along and pray—but Ian could always tell his father was just doing it to make him happy.

When Gomer finally died it was at a ripe old age and when Ian prayed for him, prayed for his safe voyage in the hereafter, inevitably, it was often the Calf that he saw.

"Don't think of the Calf," he would say to himself, but the harder he prayed and thought about trying not to think about the Calf, the more the Calf would enter his thoughts and prayers. After some years had passed, Ian eventually got used to the intrusions and stopped trying to fight them. In his mind, he looked upon the golden man-headed cow, or the cow-headed man, and he just prayed the best he could.

Samson and Delilah

Samson's father was an Israelite named Manoah. Manoah was an intellectual who referred to himself as a "man of peace." He believed the troubles between his people and the Philistines could be solved through nonviolence, so when a Philistine baited him— smacking him in the back of the neck—he would look at his tormentor with this "I pity you" look on his face. In this way, he felt he was initiating social change.

But his son was not naturally given to thoughts of peace. Punching and throwing things around was Samson's natural way. It wasn't that he was bad; it was just that he was blessed with a great strength that needed continual venting. It was always that way. During his first few seconds of life, he bit the midwife's finger with a force that caused her to bleed and cry out, "That little bastard." At five, he could chop wood with the side of his hand, and at seven, he was able to wrestle a horse to the ground. For Samson, acts of brutishness were like what whistling was to a musical genius—something deep inside that had to come out. Kicking a camel in the stomach and watching it fall to its knees was like hitting a high C.

Manoah was embarrassed by his son's feats of strength. He found them oafish.

"If you sat down and read a book, then I would be impressed," his father said.

When he was growing up, Samson wanted to be an angel. Partly it was because he thought it might make his father like him more, but also because he had heard about the feats of strength that angels pulled off— shoving an elephant off an old man's foot, etc.—so being an angel seemed like the best of both worlds. You could kick ass in the name of peace.

His mother had told him about a nice angel she'd met just before he was born.

"What is your name?" his mother asked the angel.

"It's nothing you can pronounce," the angel said.

The angel then told his mother that she would give birth to a special boy who would be as strong as a mountain.

"That's what he said," swore Samson's mother. "A mountain."

At the age of twelve, Samson went to the market with his father and found a man's money purse on the ground. Samson scooped up the purse and riffled through it. Suddenly, his father was upon him, producing a little stick, which he broke over his son's skull.

"I wasn't stealing," cried Samson.

Samson did not know if that was true or not. He hadn't had time to think. People were looking at him. His head was hurting. He wanted to lift his father in the air and dash him against the earth. It was not the kind of thought that angels had.

Samson began thinking less and less about being an angel and concentrated more on what he was truly good at. As an adult, when he looked back upon the day at the market, he would think that that is how you become a certain way. That is how you become who you are. He would not think this thought with sentimentality. He would think it matter-of-factly, while biting into a stick of celery.

At fifteen, Samson had a friend named Jason. Jason was a Philistine but he and Samson got along just fine. Jason was always full of helpful advice. He told Samson that it wasn't enough to perform feats of strength. You had to distinguish yourself. He told Samson he would need a catchphrase. Jason made a few suggestions: "Bring on the pain," "Load me up, boys," and "I am stronger than a tree trunk, and you?"

"Any schmuck can yank a crocodile's tail off," said Jason, "but to make the people love you—that's a gift."

When working on gimmicks, the first idea that came to Samson was to grow his hair long. His mother, when recounting the story of the angel, would sometimes say he told her Samson was going to be a Nazarite. A Nazarite was a kind of holy man who was not allowed to touch dead people, drink booze, or cut his hair. The angel had told her all kinds of other things, too, most of which she had forgotten, but Samson's mother had resolved to raise her son like a proper Nazarite.

Samson's father, who did not have much use for God and superstitions, had attributed his wife's angelic vision to an attack of the nerves. He refused to have his son go about with the hair of pony.

There was one summer, though, when Samson was in his thirteenth year, when his father was away traveling on business, that his bangs got long enough to fall into his eyes. He liked the way they felt there. He liked blowing them out of the way, because it gave him something to do when people looked at him. He wanted to keep growing his hair until it reached his chin, but when his father returned, he told Samson that he looked like a girl. Samson told his father that he did not care and his father slapped him in the nose.

So now, two years later and quite full grown, Samson decided to grow his hair once again. This was in the days before barbarians, and it was not common to see a long-haired warrior. Fighters and strong men commonly kept their hair short because they tended to crack things against their skulls, and, aesthetically speaking, it was more pleasing to see a brickbat shatter against a clean scalp.

As the months wore on, Samson took great satisfaction in the growth of his hair. Seeing it get longer really made him feel like he was doing something; and it might have only been his imagination, but he did feel stronger. And who in his right mind would accuse him of looking like a girl now? His biceps were the size of thighs and his thighs the size of watermelons. He cracked pecans between his pectorals! His fingers, when rigid, were as lethal as daggers. (He had once stabbed a pig through the neck with his pinkie finger, and the shock of how soft and wet it was in there caused him to withdraw with a high-pitched yip that shocked the gathering crowd.)

In his father's presence, he tied his hair back in a bun. Manoah thought it made Samson look like a certain great-aunt of his, a sour-faced unenlightened woman whom he never could stand.

When Samson was eighteen he met a young Philistine named Delilah. She worked at the market selling eggs and knickknacks. Delilah was a class act. She was demure!

"One must be careful with eggs," she would say in a hushed voice. "They are the fragile heart of the world."

When Delilah danced and her skirts rose into the air, for Samson it was like God was saying, "ta-dum." It was like the whole world was nothing, just a joke, and the only thing that mattered was Delilah's legs. He adored her so much that he sometimes pretended he *was* Delilah. He said things that he could imagine Delilah saying, things that he thought were intelligent and poetic.

"Eggs," he would say. "They make a mess when they fall on the floor."

He thought about Delilah all the time. Sometimes he thought about her so fiercely that it felt as if his mighty head was going to crack right down the middle. He found himself buying sixty to seventy eggs a week and pretending it was Delilah who had laid them, that she had kept each egg warmed beneath her buttocks, waiting for Samson to taste them. Eating her eggs made him feel close to her. He would crack each one into his mouth and let it leak down his throat.

When he saw Delilah, mostly all he could do was smile because when he spoke, only nonsense came out. Yet when he was alone in the fields near his home, he grew bold. He would swear his love to her while holding on to the bangs of his hair with his fists. "I love you, Delilah," he would say, his arms wrapped around a tree. He would say it over and over, getting a little louder each time until the tree snapped. Speaking those words made him drunk.

Eventually, Samson came up with an idea to win Delilah's heart: he would show up at the market and perform feats of strength. He and Jason would set up the operation directly across from her stand, and all the while, as he performed, he would look her right in the eye. A part of him felt like it was a pretty immature thing to do, but he didn't know what else he had to offer and he had to do something.

So Samson would drag a baby elephant to the market and struggle with the poor animal until he had it raised over his head. As he performed, people gathered around to watch. He would scan the crowd to make sure his father was not present, then he would stick out his stomach and try to get his footing right. Next, he would haul the calf over his head and look right at Delilah, to see what she made of the whole thing. As Samson looked at her, he tried to fill his mind with the greatest, most beautiful things so that maybe she would see greatness and beauty in his eyes. As he watched her, the elephant held high in the air, he thought about running his hands up her legs. He thought about kissing her.

He continued his act in the market and it turned into a nice gig. At the end of each day he would hand all of the money he earned to his father and his father would just stare at him blankly as though deep in thought about something of a geopolitical nature.

Samson often wondered what it was that made a man strong. As big as he was, there were men who were bigger, yet he was the strongest. There was just something inside him that pushed harder than anyone else. But what was that something? Was it an angel? An angel that was struggling to get himself out of there? An angel that was dying of frustration?

Yes, he was strong, but he was not as strong as people thought he was. The crowds who gathered to watch always figured Samson was holding a little something back. Holding something back was the way of the strong man. The strong man doled out a feat of strength here and there, always keeping you guessing. He made you feel like his greatest tour de force was yet to come, careful not to blow his load too soon. The truth was, though, that Samson had nearly given himself a hernia when he lifted up the platform of twelve men. In the middle of the performance he felt his balls drop and his spine become an uncertain worm. If Delilah had not been present, he would have started crying.

Samson talked about Delilah to his friend Jason all the time. He told him Delilah was a peephole to God, that Delilah was what music looked like. He tried to get Jason to agree.

"She's alright," Jason would say.

Samson begged Jason to tell him stories about Delilah because Jason was a storyteller. Jason invented long, complex epics about her, the things that she ate, the places she went. Samson would get all excited. He would lie on his stomach, his feet crisscrossed above him.

One day, Samson decided to start sending Jason to Delilah's. He was too shy to speak with her, but Jason had a gift with words.

"Go forth and tell her of the deeds of good strength

I have performed to honor her. Speak of the falcon whose beak I bit off, but make it sound like poetry."

Jason, who loved Samson, did as his friend bade him. While he sat with Delilah, he would play his lyre. He would make up songs about the great things that Samson did.

"You play *some* lyre," said Delilah.

As their visits together went on, Delilah and Jason saw that they had a great deal in common. They both loved traditional Philistine folk ballads and found avocado pits, when clutched in one's hand, to be of inexplicable comfort. They began to speak less of Samson, and more of Jason and Delilah.

While Jason was with Delilah, Samson waited anxiously, curling great weights to pass the time. When Jason returned, Samson would ambush him.

"What did she say?"

"She is mightily impressed," said Jason.

"Does she love me yet?"

"No, but she likes you, though. A lot. As a friend. She told me that underneath all the tough-guy antics you're probably a big softy."

"That is true," said Samson. "What else did she say?"

Jason looked at him for a couple seconds.

"She said she loves me. I love her, too. We want to get married."

Samson took a moment to consider Jason's words, and then, as matter-of-factly as he would lace up a sandal, he wrapped his long hair around Jason's neck and strangled his friend to death.

It was after killing Jason that Samson started to change. He moved out of his father's house and became less satisfied lifting and maiming animals. He felt it was time to move on to people. Philistine people. Some Israelites had approached him in the past about leading their uprising.

"You're a Jew, Samson," the emissaries would tell him. "Come let us conquer the land of the uncircumcised."

"No, thank you," Samson would say. "I have no beef with the Philistines. They treat me just fine, and make great music."

He knew his father would fly off the handle if he saw Samson so much as *talking* to one of those "uprising" guys.

Now, though, he decided he wanted to deliver the Jews. When asked about the change of heart, he would say, "Personal reasons." Samson was not a political animal. He just wanted to hit people, hard enough to make them die. It would be like making Jason die again and again. Once was not enough.

News of Samson's God-like power spread like wild. He was no longer a sideshow. He became famous. Men would pat his arms, nod, and say, "Nice," while women longed to know him in the biblical sense. It was rumored that even when Samson's penis was half flaccid, it was strong enough for a woman to perch on like a bird on a branch.

Samson, for his part, spent most of his leisure time just sitting back and pondering all that he could kill. He'd look upon a man or beast and think of how long it would take to rob the creature of its life. Old man— four seconds; bear—three-quarters of an hour. At night he would dream of pushing his foot right through the chests of the Philistines and removing it like he was taking off a leather slipper.

Killing became a kind of therapy for Samson. *This one looks like that teacher who called me lunk-headed; this one looks like my father.* He lifted that man up to his face by the beard so he could spit in his eye. At such times, Samson felt like he was working things out.

But his murdering only exacerbated his problems, which only made him more murderous. He felt like he was chipping away at one big enemy, but the more he chipped, the bigger it grew.

It was while Samson was in the market of Timnath buying ointments to apply to his massive, battle-wearied muscles that he met up with Delilah. She was on a road trip and was buying bread.

"Samson of the long hair," she said, sneaking up beside him. "How goes it?"

He felt his great skull-sized knees start to buckle. It was as though something inside him that he'd thought was dead had crawled out to face him. An angel. He stood before her, stammering, until Delilah smiled and told him she had a splinter and would he be so kind as to carry her to her inn.

Samson's hands floated out from his sides. He placed his thumbs under Delilah's armpits, which were warm and soft. He lifted her slowly off the ground until she was eye level with him. He walked forward like a somnambulist, staring into her eyes without blinking. She giggled and told him not to be silly, and he placed her on his shoulders. She spread her legs wide around the back of his tree-trunk neck and rode him in silence. After a while, she gritted her teeth, swallowed hard, and ran her hand through his knotted hair.

She knows all that I think, Samson thought. *Even now. And even now. And now still.*

The first time they made love, Delilah felt like she was being dug away, that when he was finished there would be nothing left of her. Samson smelled like live chickens and saliva. The tips of his greasy hair poked her face.

When he was done, Samson lay beside her, his hands behind his head, exposing his armpits.

"What is the secret of your strength?" asked Delilah. She said it quickly. She was impatient. She wanted revenge for Jason's death. She wanted revenge for her people—all of this before passing out from the stink of him.

Samson considered telling her the story of his mother

and the angel, but he did not want to get all serious so fast. He was aware of how intense he could be, and he decided to keep it in check. He knew that once he got started, he would never be able to shut up, pouring out his heart about everything: how he hates his father, how he can't stop thinking about Jason, how he's loved her so long that he feels, at this moment, like he could simply die of happiness. Just thinking about all those things, how true they were, made him feel like he was going to cry. So instead, he tried to be playful.

"I do not know the source of my strength, but I do know that if I were ever made the marshal in a parade, that would be the end of it."

"Who told you this?" asked Delilah.

"An old weird-looking woman," said Samson. "She had a limp."

That evening Delilah met with her cohorts at the tavern. She told them what she had learned.

"It makes sense," said Delilah. "If we honor him, it will throw a ray of light onto him and the gods will become jealous."

"Killing a thousand men in battle hasn't gotten the gods' attention?" asked Delilah's brother Potifar.

The Philistines arranged for a parade to honor their

mighty enemy. There was to be a marching band and even a banner that would read, "May the gods anoint Samson." There were to be lyre players, snake charmers, mimics, and women gyrating their hips.

They marched to Samson's front door, whereupon Samson moved swiftly among their ranks, from musician to juggler to belly dancer, slaughtering indiscriminately using only his feet, fists, and the jawbone from the ass he was in the midst of munching.

"Let the smiting rain down like morning dew," cried Samson, twirling two old men around by their chin fat.

Delilah turned away from the slaughter and looked up to the heavens. It was a clear, cloudless day. She was wondering if her family had made it away safely when she saw Samson stop dead in his tracks in front of her.

"What are *you* doing here?" he asked.

The next morning, Samson showed up at their love nest, a bullock draped over his shoulder like a shawl.

"I brought us some grub," he said.

Delilah watched Samson tear into the animal.

"You know, during your attack you broke my grandfather's hip."

"What did he look like? I never forget the face of one I have punished with my fists."

"He has white hair. He looks like an old man."

"Does he scream like a girl? There was an old-timer who had screams that tickled my ears."

Killing people was making Samson more numb by the day. He liked it that way. He wanted to get so numb that he would no longer be able to hear the voices of the people he had killed, which haunted him nightly, or the chastising voice of his father, who had disavowed and disowned him. Even when he thought back to the last time he saw his father, out in the market, and how the old man had slapped him across the lips in front of everyone, he could not get worked up. The only thing that Samson got worked up about was Delilah. He would stay up all night, replaying the significance of certain words she spoke and how she spoke them. If she did not greet him with a smile, he worried that she had grown bored of him and he would babble anxiously about this battle and that—anything to keep her attention. He was greedy for every second he could have of her. For each second was a lifetime of happiness. When she touched his face, he felt like a sparrow's wing had gotten under his flesh.

Again, Delilah asked her question. She asked it angrily.

"What is the secret of your great strength?"

"It is my hatred of the Philistines that makes me strong. Aside from you, they bring out the worst in me. Just thinking about them makes my bowels watery."

"Do you mean that if you did not hate the Philistines you would lose your strength?"

"Who knows?" said Samson. "Anything's possible."

Delilah set aside her anger, which was great, in order to win Samson over with the splendor of her kinsmen.

"The Philistines are a gentle, scholarly people," she said. "My brother Potifar weeps when he sees dead birds."

"He will weep all the more when I bludgeon his skull with the heel of my foot."

"My cousin Stephan prays each day for peace," said Delilah.

"He had better pray for a speedy death, for when my sandal enters his kneeling arse he will wish he had never been born."

"My great-uncle Serge plays a panpipe that would bring tears to your eyes."

"I will make Jewish his penis with my teeth," declared Samson.

As the weeks wore on, Delilah continued to bug Samson for his secret. After he told her that carrots were his weakness, the next morning he awoke to find carrots sticking out of every orifice on his body. When he told her that it was the Earth's sun that fueled him, he awoke the next morning to find himself in a pitch-black catacomb. He had to scrape his way out with his fingernails and toenails.

It was after eleven of these unfortunate events that Samson finally allowed himself to see what was happening. It was his sick love of Delilah that had been keeping him so deluded: Delilah had to be involved in the attempts on his life. All the coincidences that had been happening lately were just too odd to dismiss.

And yet he simply could not allow himself to think that one he loved so much could possibly be acting as an agent of his destruction. What kind of unlovable monster would that make him? He pushed the thought from his head, and continued to keep deferring, offering Delilah jokes and lies instead of the truth. But, in the end, he was forced to confront her.

"Delilah, if I tell you the secret of my strength, I fear you will use it against me. I am not the smartest of men, but I do know that something is amiss."

"Pranks of the gods," she said. "Everyone—even the spirits—tries to tear us apart."

"It's just so weird," said Samson.

"You do like me?" she asked.

"I would beat myself to death with my own fists for you," he answered.

"My being a Philistine doesn't change anything, right?"

"Sometimes it makes me feel like a hypocrite, what with the way I murder you guys, but nothing could ever make me love you less."

"Would you do anything for me?"

"I would walk through walls of fire for you."

"Then tell me what makes you so strong. There is an

old Philistine saying, 'The truth will make you grow stronger.'"

Samson undid his ponytail and leaned back in bed, his hair fanned out across the pillow like the tail of a peacock.

Because of the drugs, Samson fell into a deep, deep sleep, and when he awoke, and opened his eyes and saw only darkness, his first thought was that he was buried alive again. He reached out his arms to begin scratching away at the dirt, but there was no dirt. He could feel nothing. He stood up. His head hurt. He rubbed it and felt the stubble. He closed and opened his eyes. Carefully, he started to walk. He heard a giggle and swung out his arms. Then he felt the tip of his nose burned by fire. The giggle got louder. The fire was held to his lips, and then to his fingers. In the darkness, he could feel the fire burning his skin; he just could not see it.

He reached his hands up to his eyes, but his eyes were not there. The giggles turned into screams of laughter. It was like his eyes were somewhere in the darkness, laughing at him.

When the impossible idea of his blindness finally sank in, Samson screeched like an eagle. It was like when he was a little kid and his father was beating him unjustly. He would not have ever guessed he could still make sounds like that.

Samson was only blind for a few weeks before he forgot what the world looked like. He could no longer even recall what faces were. When he heard voices, he could only envision swirling rings of gas. He lay on the ground, clutching his forehead and crying. Sometimes he thought he heard laughter. Sometimes he thought he felt a finger on his back. He would flip around and slice his arms through the darkness, touching nothing.

In the gloom, old memories clawed at him. Once when he was twelve, while out walking through the desert with his parents, a lion descended from the mountains hungry for blood. To protect them all, Samson threw himself upon the lion. Even as he risked his life, he could not resist thinking of how stupid he must have appeared in his father's eyes—rolling about in the sand, grunting through his nose. He showed no dignity. At the end of the long battle, Samson tore open the lion's stomach and revealed there to be honey inside. It was just like in a dream, how he reached in his hand and offered some to his father from the tips of his fingers. His father told him that it wasn't honey, that his hands were covered in blood. Samson looked down and saw that his father was right. He couldn't understand how he could have been so impossibly wrong about something so obvious. Often he would think his father was nearby in the darkness and he would try to keep himself from crying, but it was no use.

Even when he was a kid, Samson hated being alone. Now, in the dark, he was terrified that he would be alone forever. It was after just six imprisoned weeks that Samson pretty much lost the whole of his mind. It turned out that he was just that sort of guy.

In the darkness, he believed he was visited by God.

"You have spent your life making an ass of yourself," said the Lord, "but you have done so in a most interesting way."

God kissed Samson's forehead and threw him into the air, where Samson flapped around and turned into a light that was pure and blinding. The brightness of the light that he was made his teeth hurt. He could not turn himself off! But he was free. The angel inside him had finally escaped.

When two guards showed up and dragged Samson out the door by his feet and into the sun, he thought he was being flown to Heaven by angels. The guards brought him to the king's court, where a party was in full swing. They dragged him before the king, and they bound his arms to pillars.

"Your short hair makes your face look fat," said the king.

Samson thought that he was standing at the gates of Heaven, and that the king was God. That God would be so cruel made sense to him. He tried to kneel, but his bound arms kept him upright.

Standing there, Samson no longer wanted to think upon his old life. Now he only wanted to get into Heaven. Again he pulled at the pillars, trying to force his knees onto the ground, to supplicate himself, but his attempts were in vain.

Then he heard the sound of lips smacking. The sound

came from nearby, but Samson could not match the sound to any particular thing. It sounded like the universe was being sucked up. It sounded like the gates of Heaven were being sealed. The sound came from Delilah's lips, which were kissing the chest of her lover. She pulled herself away from his arms and stepped up to the bound man.

"I have always hated you," she told him, her mouth full of grapes.

Delilah then punched Samson directly on the belly button.

"That is for everything," she said.

Samson's eye sockets became wide, and you could see right into the blackness in his head. He lunged his chest forth and the pillars shook. They began to give, imperceptibly at first, but then, with each tug, more and more. He felt the ground beneath his feet tremble. Then he heard cracking sounds and the laughing turned to shrieking. Samson continued to thrust himself forward. He wanted to feel Delilah's touch once more.

King David

Part I: Goliath

Goliath was a Philistine giant who considered himself a laugh riot, and a part of his shtick was coming up with inventive ways to kill Jews. For instance, one time he tied the beards of five Hebrews together, dropped them in a sack, climbed a tree, and threw them from the highest branch. He called it The Fatal Hora. Another time he nailed banana peels to the soles of a half dozen Jews and paid a musician to play rapid harp music as he chased them about with a tent peg.

As well as being creative at murder, he also had a very big and hurtful mouth. He used it to make the Jews look bad. When Goliath stood on the hilltop near the Hebrew camp and called out to them mockingly—calling them Jewburgers, Jewlips, Jewy Jewballs and other anti-Semitic foods—the Jews pretended not to care. But they did care. Still, they figured it was better to endure insults than broken bones.

Goliath stood outside the camp for hours, acting like the life of the party—cracking jokes about how circumcised penises were like shrimpy mushrooms, better for making broth than satisfying the lust of a Jewess.

"I once dated a lady Jew," riffed the Philistine giant. "And after having screwed her just so, she sang me one of her postcoital Jew melodies—a plaintive tune about the teeny-balled male of her species. A Jew makes love as though trepidatiously dipping his toe into cold bathwater, while a Philistine makes love as though hungrily eating watermelon after having screwed a Jewess."

When he was done performing, he would issue his challenge. It was always the same: send over your best warrior so I can fight him one-on-one. In this way, Goliath wanted to make his battles into a kind of performance—a chance to pause and deliver zingers while issuing a Jew his licks.

"By this method," said Goliath, "we might observe how a Jew fights as though he is gingerly dabbing underdone yolk off his chin, while a Philistine fights as though he is hungrily eating honeydew after having burned down a kosher butcher shop."

Whenever Goliath made his threats, everyone pretended they couldn't hear him. They made like they were too caught up sharpening something or trying to scrub an impossible stain off their battle kilt. It helped them get through the day.

There was on this particular occasion a young Hebrew in attendance named David. David was a shepherd who had shown up to bring his older brothers lunch. He watched the kibitzing giant whoop it up and hated the demoralizing effect it was having on the Hebrew army; but even more than that, he hated Goliath's comedic material. He thought "Jews fight like this/Philistines fight like that" to be one of the lowest forms of comedy—only outdone by inventing cute names for pitching Jews from trees. David was offended by Goliath's threats and violence, but he was even more offended by Goliath's threats and violence to comedy.

Maybe he wasn't as big and tough as Goliath, but David knew for certain that he was funnier. He had to be. Out of his seven brothers, he was not the wisest, nor was he the handsomest, the strongest, kindest, smartest, or even the cleanest. Comedy was what you got when all the really good qualities were already taken. And so, David knew that, by default, he had to be funny. What else was there left him?

David was the guy who placed inflated camel bladders on chairs for family members to unwittingly sit on—the guy who once set a mulberry bush on fire and hid behind it, pretending he was the voice of God.

"Repent," he intoned to those who passed, "also hop on one foot and make duck sounds."

While Goliath got his laughs by putting people down and murdering them in complicated, flashy ways, David had a different take on what comedy could be. He believed you could achieve a humorous effect by killing someone simply, too. The time was right, he believed, for a honed-down, deadpan kind of murder/comedy. He believed a simple stone-to-the-head killing could be a comedic statement as well as a political one—a challenge to the decadent pageantry of Philistine giant murder.

And so David decided that with a mere stone he would slay Goliath. Clean and economical. And funny—laugh-out-loud funny.

He was sure that if it was done right—if his timing

was just so—killing Goliath could be a highly original goof. A little schmegeggy. A big schlub. The little one kills the big one. Bonk. Death. That's comedy.

The manner in which I kill Goliath will cause the whole world to laugh, thought David. *Even God Himself will laugh.*

David wanted to please the Lord, and he believed a hardy chuckle would do Him good.

David's love of laughter began when he was a child and he had tickled an older girl on the stomach until she had peed. At the time it had felt like a magic trick, like he had figured something out. He felt like the first person to have ever milked a goat—the shock! And the sound of her laughter—like something cracking inside her, bubbling up, coming to the top—no words, just something from the depths. It was a miracle. He remembered how everything became speeded up but the pee was very slow, the way it spread like a butterfly on the ground beneath her.

So making a joke was like tickling a girl but with invisible pinkies, which made it even better—more magical. And there could always be pee, too. It was always possible. When he slayed Goliath there could be women watching and these women could laugh. Some might laugh loudly, others quietly, and there might be a woman there who would pee. Just a few drops. But then also maybe a lot. Maybe there would be a beautiful woman there who would transform herself into a fountain to honor the wit of his murder. They might *all* pee as Goliath died. As he killed him and he died.

Of course it was not impossible that Goliath might kill him, but David did not want to think about that. He did not want to think of Goliath wrapping a vine of grapes around his penis when he was dead and pulling him around like a toy—because that was the kind of funny guy that Goliath was. David would be dead and as his soul was flying up to Heaven it would have to look down and see a thing like that. What a last thing to see! But he was not going to think about that. A slayer of giants had to be pure of intent when he did his slaying. Even a mite of doubt could foul the whole thing.

* * *

David lay in bed at night and planned it all out.

"Maybe if I strike him right in mid-insult—just after the words 'and furthermore . . .'—or pop him just as he's gulping from his goblet so the stone can bounce off his head and plop into his wine! If the Lord, in His infinite kindness, might grant Goliath's dropping dead to be preceded by a plopping sound, I will have achieved a comedy of the highest order!"

David wondered what it was going to be like to be the greatest hero who ever lived. He wondered if it would give him sad eyes. He had once seen a hero who had them. With sad eyes, women would see him and think, "What sad eyes," and then they would know that even though he kept up a brave and comical front, killing giants was not all fun, that it left a person with a certain unasked-for gravitas, that it forced you to know things that no one else could ever know and these things left you sadder. But also sexier.

When he is a funny, sad, sexy great hero they will bring him women. Sometimes two at a time. He will invite them into his chambers and sit on the edge of his bed while sipping wine. They will listen while seated cross-legged on the floor as he tells funny tales with reserved sadness and sad tales with impossible mirth.

* * *

David finally worked up the nerve to tell his brothers how he wanted to battle the giant. He did not tell them about the other stuff—with the laughing women and the eyes—but still, they were unsupportive.

"David," they said, "if you do this idiotic thing we will no longer be your brothers. You can kiss all that good-bye."

But David was fixated. He could only think of the laughter that awaited him.

For forty days Goliath stood on the hilltop and issued challenges.

"Send out your best man to fight me. If he wins, the Philistines shall be your slaves. We shall press your olives, pick your Jewberries, and listen attentively to your boring stories about God. But this will not happen. What will happen is this: I will kill your man and munch his toes like pecans. And with that little snack I will be making a broader gesture: eating the toes of all

Jews everywhere—and by toes I mean spirit—but also toes. Can you see what I am getting at?"

They could see what he was getting at, and really imagine it, too: Goliath delicately twisting their toes off one at a time with index finger and thumb, popping them into his mouth—saving the pinkie toe for last.

To ease their spirits, the Jewish soldiers returned to one of their favorite subjects—the dream match: Samson versus Goliath.

"Are you kidding me? It would have been a bloodbath," they said, getting all worked up and forgetting their troubles. "Samson would have used Goliath's size against him. He'd have climbed him like a beanpole and ripped his head off with his bare hands."

On this particular day David had again shown up with food for his brothers. It was an excuse to get in on the action.

"How can you let Goliath talk that way about the army of the Hebrew god?" David asked his brothers.

"You're being loud," they said. "He might hear you!"

David kept stirring it up, talking about how the Jews were number one and shouldn't be taking that kind of flak. Eventually, David's mouthing off got back to King Saul, who sent for him.

When David stood before the king, he told him how he wanted to battle Goliath and the king gave him his trademark sideways smirk. The smirk meant many, often contradictory, things. In this case it meant, "The kid's got style," and so, believing himself to be all for style, King Saul offered David his shield and armor to use in battle with the giant.

"I don't need that stuff," said David. "I have God on my side." In truth, David was afraid the armor would make him look more imposing than he needed to be, and thus ruin the comedic staging of the whole little guy–big guy routine.

David produced his sling. It was just a leather strap.

"This is all I need," said David. "This and God."

"Tell you what," King Saul said, having a good time. "You kill this gigantic showboating asshole and I'll take good care of you."

Having killed Goliath so many times in his mind, it already felt like a done deal. David had been living in the future, but now he was setting out into the past to preserve the present and ensure the chuckle-filled future to come—with all the rewards a king could bestow. David did this sort of half strut out the door, swinging the sling around like a pocket watch.

Some kid, thought the king.

David approached Goliath. How stupid, he thought, to be so big. It was asinine. Imbecilic.

As the giant cavorted about, David pulled out a satchel and poured its contents onto the ground. It was vomit. As the necessary technology to produce fake vomit had not yet been invented, bringing along a bag of the real stuff was the best David could do. He thought if he could just trick Goliath into looking at it and squealing in girlish horror, it would be a good, humorous start to the battle. David kept looking down at it, even pointing—anything to make the giant notice— but it was no use. Goliath was already on a tear, playing to the audience.

"This is who you send to do battle with me?" asked Goliath. "After I have murdered him, shall I change his diapers? You Jews slay me. It's like I was telling the

Jewess cheese monger I was tenderizing yesterday evening, 'The army of King Saul is a sickly, honey cake–footed army whom you can always hear coming due to the mealy-nosed sniffling of their sinusitis.' But this little fellow is too much! He looks like something that has dribbled into a Philistine's chamber pot! Does he come with a side order of corn nibblets?"

Goliath laughed while slapping his shield carrier on the back, causing the old fellow's shoulder to become dislodged. Looking at it all from up close, David saw that the laughter Goliath caused was not real laughter at all. Goliath was a bully who produced nervous laughter. Terrified laughter. David wanted to cause laughter that made the soul brighten.

"I will feed your body to the birds and dogs," needled Goliath, interrupting David's thoughts.

"I will feed *your* body to the birds and dogs," bantered David. He then looked over at the Hebrew army to see if they were laughing at his rejoinder, but they just stared at their feet.

"I will feed *your* body to the birds and dogs," Goliath asserted, this time underlining the word "your" with such force that David could smell his deadly breath from across the battle plain.

"You win," quipped David, "but you still might want to chew on a mint leaf."

"I shall chew on your still-beating heart," parried Goliath.

"Do you kiss your brothers with that mouth?" asked David.

"Enough playing the dozens," growled the giant. "Now we fight."

David carefully placed a stone into the sling and swung it around. The two or three times he had practiced with the sling he had seen that whenever he twirled it, he could not help swirling his hips in a highly provocative manner, and so he tried to keep his belly dancing under control. He did not want to be handing Goliath material on a silver platter. Finally releasing, the plum-sized rock sailed through the air and hit the giant square in the center of his forehead. Goliath fell backward onto the ground. A few soldiers looked up from their feet, but they did not laugh. They seemed glad—glad and nervous—but they didn't actually laugh. No one did.

What's going on? thought David. *Soon the laughs will start.*

But there were no laughs. Not a snicker, a stifled

snort or even a "Man, that's funny." Nothing. And right away, David knew that he had erred. His timing had somehow been off—not exquisite enough. Perhaps he had been overzealous in his delivery of the stone. Perhaps slings and stones just weren't funny. Maybe he should have tricked the giant into walking off a cliff, or running at top speed into a temple wall. Why would he have thought that a little pisher killing a giant with a sling would be a powerful joke to make God laugh? How could he have gotten such an ignorant idea into his head? If he had only just slapped him over the head with a scourge handle!

When the Hebrew army saw that Goliath was really dead, they let out a cheer.

"Little David has destroyed the giant," they cried.

They knew David's feat was important, possibly even a miracle, but they did not laugh. David was nauseous.

"Go on and cut Goliath's head off," his brothers shouted, for that was the custom back then when one slaughtered a giant. But David's heart wasn't in it.

There will be no more jest-making, he thought. *No more wine bibbery or hay making.*

He just wanted to go home.

I will never trust another thing that comes from my head

or heart, he thought. *From now on I listen only to God.* And with this vow, he set himself to the sloppy job of beheading the giant with halfhearted chops.

Once the head was severed, David hefted it up in his arms and, with great awkwardness, cradled it to his chest. It was almost as large as his entire upper torso. He positioned the face so that the eyes, still wide open, appeared to be looking up at him. It was in that moment, as he stared into Goliath's eyes, that David was seized with a divine thought. A divine comedic thought. Placing his fingers on the dead giant's lips, he moved them up and down.

"Hello," David said, lowering his voice several octaves. "I am Goliath's head. Has anyone seen my hands for I wish to scratch my ass. For that matter, has anyone seen my ass?"

A joker must joke, David surmised. He looked up into the crowd and out of the stunned silence, he thought he heard a giggle. David looked back down at Goliath's head and went on with the show.

Part II: Bathsheba

As promised, King Saul rewarded David for his bravery. He was to give David his daughter Michal's hand in marriage.

"But first," said the king, "you must bring me the foreskins of one hundred Philistines."

"What does a person need with one hundred foreskins?" asked David.

"Let me worry about that," answered the king.

"Because it's not the most romantic way to start a marriage."

The truth was that Saul had devised the impossible foreskin quest as a way of killing off the brave young Jew. After his performance with Goliath, David had become very popular among the people and Saul was jealous.

Just the same, David, now a full-on war machine fueled by the Lord, killed *two hundred* Philistines and brought King Saul their foreskins. Saul received the dripping, stinking bag with his trademark smirk; but this time it was turned downward, as though he were being held upside down by the ankles.

More than he wanted Michal's hand in marriage,

more than he wanted riches or fame, David yearned to make people laugh.

"Here's a joke," he announced. "A Canaanite, a Hittite, and an Amorite walk into a temple. The Canaanite, being a Canaanite, possesses a polluted soul and being in a house of worship causes him to fall to the ground and die. The Hittite, being a Hittite and having a proclivity for baring false witness, accuses the Amorite of murder. The Amorite thus slays the Hittite. He then says a prayer for both men. Years later the Amorite does not remember either of the men's names."

For David, laughter was the one big holy—that which awakened the soul to the divine and the true and in this case, what was divine and true was that Amorites had poor memories and Canaanites were the scum of the Earth. To be reminded of this was to slap one's knee with good cheer.

After his whole performance with Goliath, David was no longer content to be funny through violence. There was nothing wrong with a little physical comedy—the whole little guy–big guy routine was a classic, but it was also pretty unreliable. David now wanted to be funny with words and, when the situation presented itself, ventriloquism.

The only problem was that now that he was a military leader, he just never seemed to have the right opportunities for making mirth.

On his wedding night David told Michal a joke.

"Here's a joke: You know how old people always say how life goes by too fast? Well, people also say that when you are waiting in line, it is as though time hardly moves at all. So why don't we make all the old people who are ready to die stand in line? Life will then pass so slowly that they might have the illusion of staving off death indefinitely."

Michal did not respond. Not with words or with laughter. Several minutes later the newlyweds had dry, mechanical sex.

When David told Michal jokes she never laughed. The best he ever got was an "Oh, that's cute." Or a "You're so weird."

Daughter of the king or not, thought David, *the girl has no sense of humor.*

In short order David became unsatisfied and so in the evenings he played harp and tried to keep his eye on the prize. As the years wore on, he took for himself several more wives, none of whom "got" him or his jokes; but one made a delicious horehound-spiced camel cheese, and another played a shofar that sobered him down to his toes and so for David, that had to be enough.

David was becoming the most popular and successful military chief in the king's army. He was clearheaded, confident, and able—so able, in fact, that as Saul started to get old he chose David, rather than his own son, to succeed him.

The passing of the crown was not a simple business, though. Saul could not help constantly trying to murder his would-be successor.

"The way your dad is always trying to kill me," David complained to Michal, "it's so undermining."

It was only after trying to assassinate David for thirty days running—once by restringing his harp with poison vines—that Saul finally gave up and gave in to the whole we-love-David vibe. After all, if the Lord was with him, the Lord was with him, and Saul, like everyone else, needed to keep on the Lord's good side. It just made good business sense.

David proved a good king, and what made him so

good was how little being the king meant to him. Even being a good king wasn't as important to David as being a funny king. And so he tried to make jokes to the people, and the people laughed, but they laughed out of fear. He could tell. They laughed the way people had laughed at Goliath's jock jokes.

David dreamed of one day going out disguised among the citizenry to tell jokes and see if he was really funny, rather than just scary. It would be a pleasant way to pass the afternoon. He could find out how people felt about him in general.

"What do you think of King David?" he would ask an old man.

"He sure ain't no King Saul," the old man might answer.

But he never seemed to have the time. There was so much to do as a ruler and most of it was very unfunny business.

That's what happens, he thought. *Gone are the carefree days of slaying giants. As you get older you strip away the things you don't have time for, and then you are left only with the things you have time for. Your life gets skinnier and skinnier until you wonder why you go on. You go on because there are things that must get done. You become no longer a person so much as a place, an unfunny place where things come to get done.*

And in this way, the place called King David lived its life until one day, while meditating on his palace balcony, David's heart made itself known to him. He saw a woman bathing on the roof of her house. She was naked, except for her sandals, which somehow only made her seem more naked. She was the nakedest, most beautiful person David had ever seen.

He said to himself, "One day I shall marry this naked sandaled woman who stirs my heart to life." He had heard the story of how his father had met his mother, and that was how it had all started: His father had made a simple pledge to himself. It was from there that the courtship proceeded. David had always wanted to say this thing to himself, too, but he never had. When he was ten or so he used to look at girls while saying it under his breath for practice, just for fun, but then his life went by and he never got the chance to say it for real. And now here he was, saying it for real. The only thing was, the woman on the roof was already married to a soldier in David's army, a Hittite named Uriah. David had missed his chance. Everything was too late.

* * *

The woman's name was Bathsheba and after seeing her bathing, a strange thing happened. King David went to bed fully upraised, and when he woke up he was still upraised. He was to stay this way, crisp and yearning, for one hundred days.

At the end of the first day he thought, *What a story to tell our grandchildren one day,* but by the end of the week, he thought, *Schmuck, what's the matter with you?* No matter what he did—long cold showers, ball leeches, imagining his mother-in-law shucking corn in the nude—his staff would not crumble.

"This attraction is supernatural," he lied to himself, "and sanctioned by God."

During those one hundred days, David kept mostly to himself, trying to figure it all out. The more he thought about it, the more he could not stop thinking about it. Was she aware how sexy wearing only sandals made her appear? Did it make her *feel* sexy? His thoughts fed off each other, each thought provoking more thoughts, and each thought making his hardee-har-har hardier. It was endless. He thought and thought and did so while masturbating with great vigor.

It's okay to self-serve, he thought. *It keeps me from hurting anyone. It allows one to build a perfect universe made of Bathsheba, and then enter it. Wishing cannot make something so, but wishing while fisting the pharoh comes close.*

When David had to receive company he remained seated behind a table. If he had to go somewhere, he did so while walking hunched over, carrying a harp. No one asked any questions, which was one of the good things about being the king.

He didn't know what it was about her. Maybe it was the way she bent over, her legs pressed so tightly together. Maybe it was the look on her face, the tip of her tongue stuck out, touching her nose in concentration, like washing her leg was a very intellectual undertaking. Maybe it was the way her mouth always seemed just about to blossom into a smile—in response to some joke, yet untold, that David would one day tell her. He was able to remember her face so well, too. There were some people who he'd meet over and over and was still never sure if he knew them or not. But her face was burned into him. When he closed his eyes there it was, like the sun.

In his mind he wore her sandals like a mask. He was convinced that smelling Bathsheba's footwear would reveal some great, unimaginable truth—a filthy, sexy truth that would change his life forever, but in spite of his furious determination to manually self-know, there were still things about her that he could not know. Just the same, his desire to know drove him to obsession.

At night, he thought about Bathsheba's sandals. He thought about her feet, too. The idea that Bathsheba had something as mundane—as common—as toes was enough to make him swoon. From the roof he would watch her do laundry and while looking at her face, he would think about her pinkie toes—so human, so tiny and vulnerable.

At night he dreamed her baby toe had come to life. Freed of the body, all by itself, it came to him. He had willed it to visit through the force of his desire.

In the dream, the baby toe's name is Goldberg. Goldberg crawls in under the door as David is lying in bed.

"Am I catching you at a bad time?" Goldberg asks.

David recognizes him immediately.

"For Bathsheba's baby toe it is never a bad time."

He bends down onto the floor and scoops the little tot up in his hands. He squeezes and rubs him. He brings Goldberg up to his nose. He inhales. Goldberg giggles. He brings him closer, to the outside rim of his left nostril. Goldberg smells like the ocean. David pushes him into his nostril like a cork.

Suddenly King David was awake, asphyxiating.

He caught his breath and rolled over. He kissed a wife's shoulder, trying to regain his footing in the world.

In the dream he possessed a love for the toe that was stronger than any he had ever felt for anyone. If offered, he would give up his kingdom to lick the morning dew from under its nail. Unfortunately, no one was making such an offer.

The day he appeared on her roof, he got there before she did. When she saw him, she did not drop her laundry. She just did this thing with her head where she turned it to the side and laughed. Like she was embarrassed. Like she had just been thinking about him. Like the whole world knew what she was thinking. It was a weird thing she did with her head. It was spasmodic, like them just being in the same world together, breathing the same air, was too sexy not to get the shakes.

"Are you here for Uriah?" she asked.

He knew Uriah would not be there. Uriah was away in battle. "It isn't for Uriah that I come," he said. Standing there talking with Bathsheba, David realized he had not been so exhilarated since his confrontation with Goliath.

He was about to say "Here's a joke," for he had planned out in advance many jokes to tell—to get things started—but things started without jokes, and they started very suddenly.

As they did it on the roof she kept her sandals on. He watched it, the left one, as he moved back and forth within her, and as he was just about to end it all, he grabbed her sandaled foot to his face and drew in a sharp breath. He could smell nothing.

Again, his heart had fooled him. But it was too late: David had made her pregnant.

What choice do I have now? thought David.

Uriah had to be removed from the picture. This David knew.

When David took Bathsheba for his wife, God was displeased. The prophet Nathan had told him, "Heads up: this thing you did with Bathsheba—God hates it. A lot." It was the way David had gone about it—sending her husband Uriah to the front, to certain death, just to get him out of the way.

In the first weeks of his illegitimate baby's life, David spent all of his day praying. He prayed so hard he felt like his head was going to explode. He prayed like he was a little kid pounding on a door screaming his head off. Then the pounding turned to scratching and the screaming turned to hyperventilating, and still he prayed, folded on the floor, his chin pressed into his chest. When the baby died he stopped praying. He didn't even say kaddish, and when those around him asked why, David asked back: What is the point? He had prayed to change God's mind, but now it was over and no amount of prayer could change that.

*   *   *

In David's grief, he became backward-looking, spending a lot of time caught up in the old days, thinking about girls he had made laugh and giants he had slain. Bathsheba's father had been there the day David had killed Goliath and he would tell Bathsheba about it. As a young girl, she never got tired of hearing the story. David and Bathsheba spent a lot of time talking about it, too. But after the baby died, the tone of these conversations changed.

"When your father told the story," David asked, "did you think it was funny, a little?"

"Funny?" she asked. "Funny how?"

"Like a little guy bonking a big guy?"

"I don't see what's so funny," she said.

"Maybe it was how he told it."

Bathsheba ground her teeth and David continued.

"Did your father say that David slew the giant, or did he say that David and God slew the giant or did he just say that the giant was slain?"

"I don't remember," she said.

David began to ask another question, but Bathsheba told him to stop dwelling. David responded by telling her that all of human history is dwelling and that without dwelling there is nothing and as David spoke, Bathsheba ground her teeth.

David had hoped that Bathsheba, unlike his other wives, might one day come to find him funny, but because of the rocky start to their marriage, there was never any room for jokes. He still hoped that one day, from out of their grief, there might grow a certain comedy and on some days, David believed that routines were already starting to take shape—routines that would eventually help them to speak through their sadness. One of these nascent routines was the drinking routine. In it, David and Bathsheba eat olives. While he chews each one carefully, she pops them by the fistful. David says she shouldn't do that because she could choke and die and Bathsheba asks, So what? David says, Oh, nothing. Then there is the sound of chewing. Then she laughs. Then he laughs. Then she stops laughing. David continues to laugh. David continues still. And so on, until she tells him to shut up. David says, Why would you say something like that? He is not sure if he is breaking character. She says nothing. David says, Eh? And again, she tells the King of Israel to shut his royal hole. He says that he doesn't like that, that someone might overhear her.

Eventually these routines would blossom into something quite hilarious.

David began to keep mostly to himself, spending a lot of time with his war souvenirs.

He still kept Goliath's head on a shelf.

"You should think about getting rid of that thing," said Bathsheba.

"It's not the kind of thing you can get rid of," said David.

"It stinks. I can't even clean near it without gagging."

Bathsheba came to know David very well and she used this knowledge to push his buttons.

"When you killed Goliath," Bathsheba asked, "how much do you think God was helping? Did he use a pinkie or did he use a fist?"

"Hard to say. I really had my eye on his forehead.

Right on the spot I hit. What the world saw as a single shot was really the product of years of great training."

"I heard that Goliath in his prime was a whole other story," she said. "By the time you guys tangoed he was fat from too much drink and obsessed with entertaining his troops with repartee."

David nodded his head, as though considering what she was saying. In his mind, though, he was pitching her off a roof.

"I heard he really wasn't that bad," Bathsheba went on. "That he was mostly talk. That he did a lot of work with lame Philistine children."

It was all about timing. If someone called you a name, said that you were a bad king, cared more about committing adultery than ruling, you could pause a beat. Pause two beats or even three. Pause an entire evening of beats. Even two days of beats. Then, after all your beats, show up at their door with an army and brain them with a stick. That is comedy, your face a grimace of satisfaction. But with your wife, all you have is what is in your mind.

"Because you know," Bathsheba continued, breaking his train of thought, "you're not just a little schmo when you have God on your side. When you stop and think about it, it was poor God-less Goliath who was at a disadvantage, no?"

Her body draped over your shoulders, slowly being lifted over your head, her sandaled feet kicking, and then over, off the roof and into sweet oblivion. These were not funny thoughts and David did not want to be thinking them, but there they were, as real and powerful as his memories, or his belief in God.

David did not know what to say.

"Here's a joke," he said, his mind a complete blank.

Part III: Absalom

David began to see that ruling the nation was affecting his chops negatively, so he summoned his royal coterie before him so that he could have someone with whom to kibitz.

"God wants to make a universe," he began. "He then makes a universe and the universe is everything, right? Everything that there can be. So where is God? Inside his own creation like a carpenter who climbs into the coffin he has made?"

Titters. A half swallow.

David began to see that he would never be able to be both a joke maker and a king. The problem was, he thought, that you are only given one life.

At first he thought a sidekick might help, some minor dignitary—an adviser with a humorous stutter—someone to play off of, but whenever he thought he had found someone, they would say the wrong thing, mess with his timing—start to showboat—and he'd end up having to beat them across the back with his scepter.

David was too out of touch with the concerns of the citizenry. He lived such a privileged and isolated existence that the things he thought were funny were actually mean and bizarre—or funny only to other kings, and he was at war with almost all of them, so that wasn't good for much.

Pacing back and forth across the palace floor, he would ask, "What's up with those guys you pay to wipe your ass?"

Besides, people just wanted to respect and fear a king, so he gave up telling jokes in favor of talking about jokes. David felt that his greatest comedic contributions might be made as a theoretician—a man who could impart his ideas *about* comedy to the next generation of jesters, clowns, merrymakers, tipplers, and want-wits. He also wanted to spend as much time away from his wives as possible.

"In the caveman days," he would instruct, "there was much pain and violence. Man had to develop a way to make himself feel marginally better. 'How can we release pleasure particles to better handle the nightmare of existence?' the caveman wondered. He found that by breaking up his howls of agony, turning them into a series of ejaculatory barks—to make the 'ahhh!' into 'ah-hah-ah-hah'—it eased the pain. You see, each laugh is composed of an 'ah' and a 'hah.' By going 'ah' and 'hah' they were able to lift the unrelenting pain of their dark, bestial days into something more recreational. It is only through the godly gift of humor that man endures the horror. What other faculty allows you to turn pain into triumph? Tears of sadness into tears of laughing too hard?"

One of King David's greatest joys was having the melancholic brought before his throne. He would cure them with the gift of comedy. David would make jokes—but only for the purpose of academic example and instruction. That way, if there were no laughs, it did not punish his soul. Education became his safety net.

"Laughter is a medicine that tastes like candy," he would start by saying. The melancholic would then erupt into hysterical, panic-stricken laughter. A guard would then poke him in the ribs. "Idiot!" the guard would whisper. "Wait for the jokes."

"Hello there, sourpuss," riffed the king. "What is your problem? Don't you want to giggle? Are you afraid that if I tickle your belly with words that you will wet your toga? Well, fear is no way to live so start laughing yourself well! That's it, double over as though you have been punched in the side. Bend! Do not fear buggery. A laughing man is seldom seduced. This is because when you laugh, others are often inclined to laugh, too. Yes, they will think twice about defiling you once a giggle has become lodged like battle shrapnel in their heart."

He would then send the cured man away, laughing, weeping, wiping sweat.

"When I first started I relied on slapstick—killing giants and that—but then I moved toward more advanced forms of humor—like wordplay. Irony!" David cocked one eyebrow. "Right now I am being ironic. Observe: 'You are beginning to piss me off. I am going to pull out my Egyptian poleax and make you into a human Torah scroll.' See? Irony. How can you tell? You just have to trust your gut. Watch: 'Boy, am I happy.' What makes that statement ironic? The prefacing word 'boy'? The fact that no one is ever really happy? Or both of these things working in tandem? Irony misused can destroy the universe in the way that it is able to create as it uncreates. It creates things that are already uncreated.

"I am not kidding," he continued, cocking his eyebrow once more. "Really, I am not."

He would lean back and await laughter and applause. If it did not happen, he would send his soldiers in to coax out their chuckles. Later in bed, King David would weep.

At this time, the best thing in David's life was his son Absalom. His son's birth was one of the few occasions in which David believed his heart had not stabbed his back. His son, he felt, was the only one who truly got him. With Absalom, for the first time in King David's life, he had the comedic sidekick he had always craved. Just being around his son made David feel fifteen percent more jocular.

Absalom had long, curly hair, which he used to drape over the front of his face to play a character called "Backwards Man." He twisted his feet to the side and walked and talked backwards while David, his partner in comedy, gigglingly followed behind, repeating each punch line seconds after Absalom spoke it.

But that Backwards Man stuff was more of what Absalom considered old-timer funny—stuff to please his dad. From David's boyhood to his son's, comedy had changed. It had become more subtle, no longer something that had to spring from violence. Comedy could do your violence for you and it was an area of battle in which Absalom excelled. Through mimicry, and caricature, Absalom was always able to take his rivals down a peg.

Absalom was also a brave warrior. He had developed this move where, while on horseback, he would stretch his hair out like a clothesline and intersect it with a foe's neck. He especially enjoyed racing into battle against the wind, because of the way his hair was made to whip backward in a very flattering manner.

*   *   *

When David wasn't ruling, he would ponder all the various forms of laughter there could be. So far, he had only categorized four: laughter at your own expense, laughter at the expense of others, laughter at the human predicament, and laughter at small animals falling off tables. Absalom, on the other hand, was not one for rabbinic musings—he just *was* funny and he didn't have to think about it.

David did not resent Absalom for his gifts. He did not want to be another King Saul—bitter and jealous. So when Absalom took center stage and the people laughed, David laughed, too. It hurt his throat a bit, this laughing, but it also made him feel like a good person—so much love for his son he had, that he could look through the tunnel of his own comedic failures and offer up a royal chortle.

What David did not know, though, was that he was his son's favorite comic subject, and whenever his father wasn't around, he would test the water with the royal subjects, throwing in an innocuous jest here and there, like how David hums when he eats—just to see how it would go over. Usually people fell silent. Absalom could see they were afraid to laugh and so he leveraged their discomfort in the service of further laugh getting.

"You know who lays some stinky farts?" Absalom would ask a table full of dining guests. "The King of Israel, that's who. And when he's braced for battle is the worst. His stomach gets so bad—forget about using the outhouse when he's finished with it! I tell you, boys, it wasn't my father's stone that felled Goliath but the vapors produced by his battle-anxious colon. Peeyoo!"

Whereas at first people did not know how to respond, slowly, over time, they began to warm to Absalom's routines. Because it felt so naughty to be laughing behind the king's back like that, it often made the laughter more intense—like it came from a deeper, more hidden place inside themselves. Absalom gave them a chance to laugh at authority and it helped everyone to feel like he was a man of the people. As a result, Absalom's popularity as a chief grew.

As David got older, he began to leave more of his ruling and millitary work to his sons and other subordinates. It allowed him more time to muse upon the nature of comedy. He did so while sitting on his throne, a serious look on his face. If he could just bring his lifetime of experience—of laughing and loving—to bear, he believed he could crack the pit of what comedy was and then share it with Absalom. Such a thing would be the greatest gift a father could give a son.

One day, he called Absalom to his side.

"Comedy should help remind people of what is real," he told his son. "Everyone gets used to the way things appear, but comedy can awaken us to what *is*."

Everyone went through life pretending, and revealing this pretending was at the core of all jokes. Everyone pretends they were born with clothes on, pretends they have an understanding with God, that they're just taking some time apart, that they'll talk later. Now that David was older, he saw all of this clearly. It was, he believed, what would allow him to be even funnier.

He was, of course, wrong.

Absalom listened to his father's musings, receiving them as the babblings of an old man, for he knew what the true secret to comedy was: farts. Farts were funny, and his father's farts were hilarious.

"You know what would really surprise old King Farty-Pants?" asked Absalom to his men. "Staging a coup. Can you imagine? It will so befoul his colon that his battle stallion shall retreat in horror."

The men listened laughingly, and laughingly did they suit up and laughingly did they choose their weapons. And then, with an occasional titter, they leaned in and listened to Absalom's plan to take over his father's kingdom.

Not being firstborn, Absalom knew that even though his father adored him, he would never be made king and so he knew he had to take matters into his own hands. With the solid support of his troops, he believed he had a good chance of taking his leadership to the next level.

But despite his age and increased sentimentality, David was still a brilliant military strategist and made short work of his son's rebellion. In no time at all, his laughing supporters became frightened retreaters and Absalom was left alone.

"Do what you must," David told Joab, his first in command, as they laid down their battle plans. "But no harm must come to Absalom."

Even though Joab knew David loved Absalom, Joab loved David enough to know that Absalom would, if not today or tomorrow, eventually lead to his undoing. So when Joab found Absalom, on his horse, caught by his long, curly hair in the branches of a tree, he knew he had no choice but to act.

As he drew near, his blade drawn, Joab paused to listen to Absalom's last words.

"Tell my father he was never funny," he said.

Joab did not repeat any of this to David, for to have done so would have been cruel and Joab was not a cruel man.

Absalom's funeral was a small affair. As David stood over his dead son and stroked hair from his face, he recalled the first funeral he had ever been to. It was his grandfather's and he was ten years old. It was there that David had made his first joke. His father, Jesse, was making a eulogy. "My father is still alive in all of our hearts," said Jesse, and David cried out while pounding himself on the chest, "Wake up, Zeyde! Everyone out here thinks you're dead."

David's father had wiped away the tears from his eyes, put his hand on his son's shoulder, and smiled.

He remembered back to a time when it seemed he could not lose, a time when he was so often victorious, had God so on his side, that life became boring. It was hard to imagine that such a time had ever existed, hard to imagine that as a young soldier, he had prayed to God to let him go into battle on his own. He wanted to see what it would be like to set forth without God. He only wanted to do it once, for the hell of it.

"Just to see," he had said, his eyes closed in prayer. He did not think it would hurt God's feelings. After all, it was normal to be curious.

After the battle, when he came home, his arm dangling dead at the elbow, his eyeball crooked in the socket, and both his ears bleeding, David discovered that without God he was nothing. It wasn't even that he was a pip-squeak, or a dried-up leaf. He was nothing. No one was anything. Everything was God. He was. His enemies were. To understand this, to feel it with clarity, was to be stronger than an army of a thousand men. But it was also terrifying. It was to know that all accomplishments were unreal. It was to know that nothing mattered except God.

As he buried his son, David thought: *I will shrink and wrinkle more and more, like soup on the fire, until I am only this hard black crust. First I will be a person, then a memory of a person, then words about a memory, then a catch phrase, and then, black crust.*

After I am dead, thought David, *everything will be revealed and so there will be no more jokes, no more need for jokes, and God, because he has always loved and supported me, will take me up to Heaven where I will sit around for thousands and thousands of years. Then a million years. And I will keep going. Then one day I will go before God and beg him to kill me. And God will say, "I cannot kill you because you are already dead." And I will say I do not even remember being alive. And he will say, "What is it that you want, because whatever it is I will bring it to you." And I will say, "With all due respect, I don't think you get it. I'm sick of all this. I'm full. I've had enough. I want to be evaporated. I want my dust to be squashed like fruit flies. I don't want one tiny insect wing of consciousness to remain. I'm sick of my own thoughts." I will say this while rubbing my eyes. God will suggest I speak with Moses. "That guy*

only makes me feel worse," I will say. "I want it to be over."
And God will make this face, like, "I hear you, I hear you."

David left the burial ground and went home. When he arrived back at the palace, he sat down with a quill and parchment and tried to make himself understood—to himself and to God—for that one day in Heaven to come.

"The Lord is my shepherd," he riffed. "I shall not want—cannot want. What is there to want?"

Jonah and the Big Fish

Vito worried about his brother constantly, always nervous that Jonah wasn't going to turn out normal. All because of the penis incident.

It was as a child, while watching Jonah sleep one night, watching his face—breathing, dreaming—that it struck Vito very hard: *Just as I am me, he is he. I could have been born Jonah as easily as I was born myself.* And how did he punctuate this epiphany? By touching Jonah's penis. Right on the tip. And as he did so, Jonah's eyes popped open. In the darkness Vito's other me stared at him blankly, his mouth hanging open.

The way he remembered it, before that moment

Jonah had always been normal. Normal. Not normal. It was like pushing a button. A penis-shaped button.

Vito was the brother who left the womb first. "I should have left a note. 'Stay put. This whole outside world thing—not for you. For you it will only be delusions and obliterating disappointment.'"

Their mother lived and breathed for her boys. A pious woman, she wore her babushka tied so tightly around her head that she had to speak through gritted teeth. She worried for her sons with laserlike intensity, as though worry was mystical work, a positive force that moved the planets.

"Jonah is not strong like you," said the mother to Vito before her death, "and so you must take care of him."

"Jonah is not sexy like you," said the father to Vito before *his* death, "and so you must get him laid."

The father did not overly concern himself with kids. He saw raising children as women's work and spent most of his time whore-mongering, debauching, frolicking, and making whoopee.

"You should see some of the foxes I have laid with," he'd brag to Vito. "All tens—not an eight or nine in the bunch."

Vito vowed to both his parents to do as they bid him.

And he did—yelling, "Whatsamatter with you!" right in Jonah's ear when he got too quiet. Weird, unlayable, and quiet.

On the odd occasion when Jonah did actually speak, it was always about things that stopped conversation dead.

"Do you ever see swirly circles in the air?" he'd ask Vito and the gang as they played draughts. "Sometimes it looks like everyone and everything is made of tiny swirling circles. Sometimes I can see it all so clearly, how we're all connected—by circles."

"This is what happens when you touch a brother's penis," Vito would think. "You scramble the brains."

He also feared that he might have scrambled Jonah down below, too, and so it made carrying out his father's orders harder than carrying out his mother's. But still, he tried. Like his father, Vito took pride in knowing a great many women, and he set his brother up on date after date—each one more disastrous than the last: Toga sleeves catching on fire. Swarms of cicadas. Piles attacks. But most horrible of all were the things that Jonah *said*, and so Vito chaperoned. In this way, he could constantly cut Jonah off when he began to say something embarrassing, something that might unwittingly provide a glimpse into the Yiddish circus that was their family life—accidentally reveal how their mother loved them so much she followed them around all day, hiding behind bushes to make sure they were safe. So passionate was she in her adoration that she gave their penises names. Vito's she called Raffi and Jonah's was Morris. Vito was always antsy during these dates, worried Jonah might let something inappropriate slip out.

"It's like that one time Vito touched my Morris." Who knew what he could say?

And so Vito sat on pins and needles, waiting for Jonah to say something to embarrass them both. He waited, perched like a hawk, ready to reach under the table and pinch a clump of Jonah's thigh hair to shut him up. In this way, he believed he was taking care of Jonah and helping him get laid. It was hard work.

At night after the dates, Vito felt the guilt lay heavily on his chest. It pressed down upon him with such insistence he feared he might wake up one morning under his bed—under the earth—impish little men prodding him with their pointy goat horns.

"Manhandle *our* privates," the tiny demons would scream.

* * *

The first time Jonah heard God, he knew right away that Vito would not like it at all.

"In forty days," Jonah told Vito meekly, "God is going to destroy Jerusalem."

This was all he needed. He was already working day and night to head off every crazy word that came out of Jonah's mouth. He mulled the situation over.

"Don't say you heard God," Vito corrected. "Say you *think* you heard God. There's a difference."

"I think I'm pretty sure about it, though," said Jonah.

"What did He sound like?" Vito asked.

"Like air. Like the mountains."

"Why can't you ever give a straight answer? 'He had a low gravelly voice. He drawled his vowels and had a wet *t*.' Those are answers."

"It wasn't even an actual voice. It was more like a feeling I got."

"So you *feel* like you think you heard God."

"I guess so."

And so when Jonah told people the news about Jerusalem, Vito would jump in with, "He only thinks he felt he heard God." Then Jonah would stop prophesizing, and then Vito would start talking about pomegranate crops.

Still, news of Jonah's prophecy got around. People spoke of the weird and gentle man from Gath who had heard God foretell of Jerusalem's doom and, to be on the safe side, Jerusalemites began to repent, but after a few weeks, with Jerusalem doing better than ever, people stopped repenting and started kibitzing.

"Sure your brother heard God," they said to Vito. "The only problem is, God lied to him."

Vito would shake his head and try to laugh in a way that said, "You win some; you lose some." But instead he laughed in a way that said, "I am sweating and humiliated." Jonah was on his way to becoming a laughingstock and Vito was going down with him.

With all this prophesizing stuff, what chance did Jonah have of enjoying a normal life?

At night, in dreams, his father looked at him expectantly.

"*Nu?*" his face said.

After the disaster of the first prophecy, years later, when God came to him again, Jonah tried to ignore Him, giving no external sign he'd heard.

"Go to Nineveh," the voice commanded. "Warn them that if they do not change their evil ways they will be destroyed in forty days."

All the while, Jonah twiddled his beard as though pondering what he might eat for lunch. When God's voice finally stopped, he ran to tell Vito what had happened.

"Again with the forty days," Vito said. "Listen to me good: You are not to go to Nineveh. You are not to tell anyone about this. We don't need another Jerusalem. To this day I can't set foot in the market without getting lip from every smart-ass with a pied-à-terre in the holy city. 'I've still got a bag packed by the door.' Jerks. Let's just sit tight on this one. Wait and see."

Jonah was to learn that God was not one for a wait-and-see attitude. For really, what was the point of prophesizing something that had already passed? And so Jonah was dogged by the Lord. When he went for a walk, the Earth spoke to him.

"Nineveh," it hissed.

"Don't listen to the Earth," said Vito. "The Earth isn't your brother."

But when the Earth did not shut up, Vito told Jonah to take to the water.

"Find a boat and set sail," said Vito. "You've never

206

been anyplace. Adventures on the open water will clear up your skin."

The idea of letting his brother wander off on his own made his heart sick. Who would stomp on his foot when he spewed gibberish? Jonah was going to float off into the world like a lonely little feather, but Vito had to let him go.

"Let God besmirch the name of someone else," he thought. "The line between prophet and false prophet is an almost invisible one."

And so Jonah set out to hide from the Lord. In spite of never having been anywhere all by himself, he did not feel alone since, secretly, he'd always felt like his dead parents were watching him. The feeling was a holdover from childhood when he actually *was* watched by his mother, who hid behind bushes and wheat piles, spying on him to make sure he was safe. The feeling of being watched was something that stuck with him all his life and since he was the kind of kid—and now the kind of man—that no one really took any notice of, it helped make him feel more like the star of his own life.

As he made his way toward the sea, he imagined his dead mother floating along with the clouds, her heart bursting with worry. It put a spring in his step.

Being alone taught him new things about himself. For one thing, without Vito there to tell him to snap out of it, he was given to much more daydreaming. His mind drifted in new directions. Allowed to flex its muscle, his imagination became fierce and powerful.

If Vito was to be believed—and Jonah trusted he was—he had always been half-crazy. Being half-crazy made him uneasy because he was never sure which was the crazy side and which was the normal. He did not have his brother's intuition for such things, so when he was uncrazy, saying things like "Fifteen silver shekels for an ox is a bit pricey," he did it with the same trepidation that he'd say "Quicksand might be a gateway to the center of the Earth—a place where rainbows are kept and if you eat one you might be able to pee in colors." On the road, Jonah stopped caring which side of him was crazy and which was not and as a result, he felt his craziness blossom, going from being the kind that chews the flesh of the fingertips to being the kind that pounds the chest and summons God.

* * *

After several days of wild imaginings and daydreams on the road, Jonah came to the edge of the water, where he saw a docked ship.

"To where is this ship sailing?" asked Jonah of a nearby sailor. He received no response, which, for Jonah, was par for the course. Buying a chicken at the market was the kind of thing that could often take up an entire afternoon with "Excuse me, sirs" and "I beg your pardons." So he simply walked on board. "Really," he thought, "it matters not where it is going, only that it is going."

On board, no one paid Jonah any mind. He wandered about the deck, touching things with his soft, moist fingers. He looked at the sky and pointed.

"Should the sky be so red this time of year?" he asked a strapping sailor who hauled rope and looked right through him.

Then with a sudden lurch, they were at sea. Through overheard snatches of conversation, Jonah learned that the boat was set for Tarshish.

"Well, then, some shut-eye it is," he said and leaned back for a snooze.

He felt that talking aloud would cheer his spirit and

allow his parents—who he suspected could see and hear him, though not actually read his mind—to know that he was all right. His mother was always one to encourage a good nap and Jonah believed that to indulge in one on board would bring comfort to her.

"Rest, rest," he imagined her saying from above.

When Jonah woke up, everything was topsy-turvy, the sailors running from stern to bow in the midst of a terrible storm. Jonah watched the action from a crouch, trying to keep out of the way. The sailors had never seen such a storm and so they knew that something was up, that God was trying to tell them something.

"He is trying to kill us—but for a reason," said one of the sailors.

"Maybe he is trying to kill only one of us," said another.

And so it was decided that to figure out who God was trying to kill, lots would be drawn. It was while passing around the little colored stones that Jonah was finally noticed.

"You there! From where did you come?"

"I was here since we left," stammered Jonah. "Remember? I even said hi to you."

It was no surprise to anyone that the lots pointed to Jonah. He looked from one sailor to the next as though to say, "Lots! The things they say!"

Before he knew it, Jonah was being carried to the side of the ship. Being carried made him feel special, like the birthday boy; but this festive feeling was only to last four seconds. At the ship's edge, panic set in.

"Wait," he cried. "Why get hasty? To be certain it's me God wants off, let's have a test."

Being a fair bunch, the sailors dangled Jonah overboard by his robe straps. The moment his toe touched water, the storm abated. As they dipped him in further, the sun popped out, and when they submerged him past his knees, little yellow birds appeared on the deck, chirping and singing. When they hefted him back onto the boat, the whirlwinds raged anew.

At Jonah's mincing request, the test was performed and reperformed a half dozen times and each time bore the same results.

"Maybe I can keep my feet dangling in the water from off the side," Jonah offered. "It would appease the irrational forces at play in the universe as well as beat the heat."

Not wanting to contaminate themselves with their stowaway's accursedness, they threw him into the water, where Jonah sank beneath the sun-dappled waves right into what appeared to be a large gaping mouth.

When he was a child, in spite of everything, Jonah had this unshakable feeling that things were going to turn out fine. And now he was in a fish. He had always felt like he was being overlooked somehow, like somehow, he didn't exist—not in the same way that other people did. As a child he had never been chased by a sheepdog. When his friends ran from them, he ran, too, but he knew in his heart that those dogs were not after him, and sometimes they would run right past him.

He worried that if he were a horse fit only for the slaughter that he'd be brought to the slaughterhouse along with all the other old horses and then, at the time of slaughtering, he would be forgotten. One by one, all the horses would be killed and he would stand in line with the rest of them but at a certain point, he would edge backward toward the door. Each passing second, he would expect to feel a tap on the shoulder, someone's—

perhaps, Babylonian—voice saying, "And where do you think you're going?" but no such voice would come. He'd make it to the door, then past the door, and then, he'd be in the town, a horse half-dead limping through the streets, past the women putting their laundry up and the boys playing ball. He would wind his way through the narrow lanes, completely unnoticed with no place to go. Not dead. Worse than dead.

His secret fear was that he had been born with only half a soul, a condition that caused him to fade in and out of being. Before he was born, when God had been filling his body with a soul, maybe He had decided to try something a little different just to keep things fresh for Himself: half man soul, half moth soul. Or maybe all morning he had been coming close to running out of souls and so He'd decided to skimp a little, pinching off half a soul from the big soul ball and then mixing the rest of it with air. The result: a Jonah soul. A person who was sometimes there and sometimes not. Vito was always there. Underlined. All in caps. Vito would have looked the fish in the face and said, "Oh, no. You're not swallowing *me*. Keep on swimming, fatso."

But with him, that fish must have just seen only water. Maybe some kelp, but no human. No soul. Nothing.

Just as he'd heard that people who jumped from mountain peaks often died of fright before hitting the ground, he now feared that he might die of embarrassment before being digested.

He wondered if the fish even knew he was in there. Did it matter? He waved his arms over his head. A squeamish guy like him had to be careful, though. Even touching something squishy and gross would be enough to get him goose-pimpled and barfing.

He supposed that if you were the kind of guy to go around cursing the day you were born, this would be the time for all that. His problem was that he did not know which kind of guy he was. He had always looked at his instincts as suspect—untrustworthy—weird. He envied guys who started off their sentences with "I'm the kind of guy who . . ." He was not that kind of guy.

As a young man Jonah would sometimes awake in the middle of the night with this feeling: that he was saddled to himself until death. Unlike every other person in the world, he could not say good-bye to Jonah and walk away. But this was close to that.

In the darkness he assessed the success of his existence: he left behind no belongings, no words to be remembered by, and no children. He had only ever kissed one person—a woman who, despite the forehead-bumping awkwardness of his lovemaking, had been kind enough to tolerate him. Vito had introduced her to him. Her real name was Eunice but Vito called her "the Macaw" because of her rapid kisses, like little pecks. Vito had brought the Macaw and him together—literally. They were at a party and his brother insisted that they sit side by side "just to see how you look together." Their legs touched. The wine flowed. Jonah put his hand on her hand. She did not shudder. Emboldened, he looked at her. After a while, she looked back. He had nothing to say. "Hi," he said.

He thought about her in the darkness and masturbated. Her tolerance, so precarious; all evening it felt like she was pulling away. *Don't go,* he kept thinking.

In the dark, in his mind, he still could not keep her from leaving. He would come before she could withdraw herself completely. It was a good way to fill his time.

On his third day in the fish Jonah awoke pretending to be oddly invigorated. He looked around with his hands on his hips. He imagined his mother watching him, her heavenly eye peering in from the spurt hole at the top of the fish. Her gaze brought out the best in him. He slapped his hands together like a camp counselor.

"I am good at being in a fish," he said. "Better than most." Then he swallowed back the date-sized lump of vomit in his throat.

"Hello! What's this? Some sort of wild berry?" It was in fact a polyp. "Praise God, who in His infinite kindness brings his loyal Earthlings manna even in the bowels of a fish!" Jonah ate one of the little purple balls, choked back another teardrop of barf, and set out to explore.

"Perhaps I can slide out between the teeth like a thread of celery," he said aloud. "But even if I could— what then? I would immediately drown! No, I am better off sitting tight."

His mother had always been a fan of sitting tight. She

had spent her whole life sitting tightly and it had served her well. She could take comfort in seeing that, despite being in the belly of a fish, her son had been raised right.

For his father, though, there would be no comfort. Amittai was a man of action—the kind of guy who would have cracked his own arm off and stabbed his way out with the jagged end. Vito and his dead father were birds of a feather. His dead father was probably gnashing his teeth over this one.

"How sad to be dead and forced to watch over this boring little nincompoop," his father was probably thinking. "I want to go see what Vito's doing. He's always up to something good."

Amittai had died when Jonah was still young. One of Jonah's only memories of him was from an afternoon long ago when he had suggested Vito and Jonah pluck dandelions in a field near their house to make a bouquet for their mother. But Jonah had been afraid to pull the flowers from the earth. He couldn't say why, then or now. There was just something about the yanking, the way the flower seemed to resist, the force and decisiveness it took to free it from the ground. It filled him with terror. Every time he tried to pull one out he became weak and nauseous.

"What is wrong with you?" asked Amittai.

Jonah sat in the sea of yellow flowers, unable to answer. He wished he could. He wanted his brain to be different. He wanted his father to leave him be. He wanted to be alone. He looked down and ran the palm of his hand along the tops of the flowers, knowing that his father was up there, looking down at him. He went on moving his hand through the flowers, embarrassed to be alive.

Jonah wrapped his body in seaweed to protect himself from the gastric acids. He made himself a seaweed purse, too, to protect the half-digested herring he'd find.

"When the purse and the body wrap match, it makes the ensemble," he said.

As hard as he tried to will himself to think otherwise, living in a fish was not a life. The cramped living quarters was one thing, but the lies one had to tell oneself!

He dropped his herring purse and finally gave in to despair. In the darkness, with tiny, pink fists, he gently pounded the great fish's uterus and wept.

"Anything is better than being in a fish," sobbed Jonah

and with these words there was a tremendous rumbling that made his teeth vibrate. He felt himself being enveloped, squeezed, and then puked onto the land. He lay on the shore watching the fish as it swam off to sea.

"She was much roomier than she looked," wept Jonah. He wiped the whale mucus and whatnot from his face, rose to his feet, and took a deep breath.

"Which way is Nineveh?" he asked the first person who passed and not only did this person look right at him, he also gave excellent directions.

Outside in the light of day, Jonah realized that the fish's digestive juices had turned all of his hair white. Jonah thought it made him look like a real prophet.

When he arrived in Nineveh, Jonah made an instant impression. News of his having been swallowed by a great fish preceded him and made everything he said seem imbued with import and pizzazz, and so when Jonah informed them that God was considering wiping them out, they repented. Jonah really got into it all, even chatting up the king.

"A fool says what he knows and a wise man knows

what he says," he told the king. "I stand before you a fool. I can only tell you what I heard. What it means is for a wise man like you to interpret."

Soon enough, the king was rending his royal vestments and wandering the streets covered in ash. And in this way, Nineveh was spared from destruction.

When Jonah got back from Nineveh he seemed different, and not just because of the white hair. He was now able to speak without gagging on his own words. Jonah answered eloquently when asked about life in the fish, and there were many people asking, for Jonah's amazing story had begun to spread far and wide. But Vito did not care much for fish stories. He worried that Jonah was now even less normal.

"He probably spent his time at sea reliving the whole penis incident," he thought.

Sure, it all *appeared* to be some matter between Jonah and God, or Jonah and the fish, but Vito knew the truth: the prophecies, the fish—all middlemen— a massive metaphor. This was really a matter between Vito and God.

* * *

No matter how much he forced Jonah to scrub, Vito could still smell fish.

"Have you tried scraping with eucalyptus leaves?" asked Vito.

"You're the only one who smells it," said Jonah.

"I'm the only one who's honest with you! Do you think those other people care if you smell like a leviathan's asshole?"

"Well, I can't smell it."

"God in his infinite mercy made it so. He who maketh all made us largely nose-deaf to our own smells. Luckily for thou, the Almighty hath made thee a brother to extract thine head from the specter of thine own ass. All of human history is divided between those who bury their heads like ostriches and those who seek reality. Praise be the Divine King for having given thee a brother who knowest reality!"

"Who will have him now?" Vito fretted. He watched Jonah as he ate his curds. "A bumbling grandfather type who reeks of sardines. Some catch. If he could just lose that openmouthed hound-dog look of retarded shock and replace it with a furrowed brow of intensity."

"Just scrunch up your bloody forehead" is what he wanted to say.

Now more than ever, Vito believed his brother needed a woman to help settle him down and so, with renewed determination, he set about arranging dates, dates that he would chaperone. If he could find a woman to touch his brother's penis, night after night—enough times to blot out his own touch—then maybe his brother would be saved.

The first date he arranged was with the Blow Job Rooster. Vito had named her this because she was always up at sunrise and rather than cockadoodledooing, she greeted the dawn with fellatio. Before you were even awake. Jonah could do worse.

"I shall introduce you to the Blow Job Rooster," Vito said. He liked saying "Blow Job Rooster," for otherwise he would have just called her Meryl, which was her name.

Before the date, Vito coached him: "Now, I don't want you starting off every sentence with 'The thing about living in a fish,' because that can become a social crutch."

Nevertheless, Jonah couldn't help himself.

"You'd be surprised by how much there was to do in there," he told Meryl. "Scooping stuff. Pulling goo from your ears. Good hygiene kept my spirits mighty."

Vito asked if he could speak to Jonah outside.

"What's with you?" he demanded. "You had a life before this. You were only in there three days."

"Being inside a fish changes people."

"Do you think you're the first person to survive being swallowed by a fish?"

Vito knew he probably was, but he desperately wanted his brother to feel just like everyone else—regular folk who'd only known the touch of nonbrothers upon their shame rods.

Back inside, Jonah kept on about life in the fish, Vito kept stomping Jonah's foot under the table, and Meryl kept wondering why she hadn't just married the nice lamp salesman from Canaan whose virtues her mother extolled.

After Jonah's disappointing date, Vito was upset.

"It's nothing to be proud of. Great fish prey on men like you because you're easy prey."

He went through his mental Rolodex: the Rump Roast Royale, Peanut Butter Mouth, Dahlia of the Stupid Comment, Locust-Winged Eyelids. Eventually a bride would be found.

"Everyone knows in principle that you're always inside God, but it still doesn't stave off loneliness. Inside a fish you don't ever feel lonely. You feel complete. Comprehended. Cared for."

"Okay, that's fine," spat Vito. "You were swallowed by a fish. You got a certificate and a handshake from the King of Gath. Get over it."

"You call it being swallowed by a fish, I call it achieving oneness with God."

"God thinks you're an idiot."

The dates continued, and so, too, did Jonah's descriptions of life in the fish, descriptions that were sweeping, painterly, magnificent, and utterly untrue.

Jonah did not concoct these stories just to impress. There was more to it than that. He wanted people to think there were happy surprises out there. Not awful surprises. Horrible, monstrous, dark, and terrifying surprises. There was no point in letting people know that there were things in life so horrid that they could fill your nights with terror and your days with running as far from the sea as possible. He would say anything that popped into his head, anything that hid the awful truth, which was that there were fish out there and, if your luck was poor enough, they would swallow you whole and there wasn't a thing you could do about it. Thinking about it was his problem and it didn't have to be anyone else's. And so Jonah lied to protect them.

"I made good use of the time, writing a memoir. The book of Jonah. It's all up here," he said, tapping his finger to the side of his head.

In truth, he had only written the first line: "Stripped of all the blubber, this is what existence is." He repeated these words to himself over and over, hoping that new words would come, but none ever did.

Contrary to what Vito might have feared, Jonah and his stories were popular and people were drawn to him and his tales. In this way, Jonah became something not un-like the first astronaut, a lying astronaut with magnificent mistruths about worlds he had never seen.

Still, Vito didn't like it. All he wanted for his brother was normalcy. As Jonah spun tales, Vito sat drumming his fingers and rolling his eyes.

"I and the fish became one," said Jonah to a woman named Lily, a.k.a. the Contradictory Redhead. Vito had nicknamed her that after she'd turned down his numerous advances. She was date number fifty-three and Vito was losing hope.

"The fish was the body, but I was the brain," said Jonah. "When I closed my eyes and concentrated hard enough, I was able to exert control. Blink, I would command. Swim, spurt, do that high-pitched shrieky sound."

"I can't take it anymore," exploded Vito. "Three days. *Three lousy days.* There's more to my brother than this! Should he be branded for life? He's just like everybody else!"

"On the contrary," said Lily. "I think being swallowed by a fish makes a person pretty special." Turning to Jonah, she continued: "You have seen something that no one else has ever seen. Describe it for me some more."

"What more is there to describe?" said Vito. "It was stinky and dark. The end."

"I guess it was dark," said Jonah, "but not in a depressing way. It was sort of cozy. And you got used to the smell and the noises after a while. It was like being in the womb. But as a fully conscious adult."

Lily's eyes were large and smiley. He had her full attention. Attention was better than tolerance. It was past tolerance. Jonah was somewhere new and bizarre. It appeared Lily actually *liked* him.

"In the center of the great fish was a giant glowing pearl. It spun slowly and caused the inside of the fish to glow. It was like a temple. I sat cross-legged and watched the pearl as it revealed to me in moving pictures the history of the sea.

"First there were water mites and they became snails and the snails went to war with each other. The snails were fierce warriors. Fierce and cruel. But then came the alligators who ate them all. Then the fish opened her eyes and they were like windows. What beauty! The unbelievable, perfect, horrible, terrifying beauty. We sank to the bottom of the sea and I saw where Moses and the children of Israel marched across the ocean's floor. I saw their footprints stamped into the mud."

Lily moved her hand to the top of Jonah's hand. He tried not to think about it too much because to think about it too much would turn his tongue into a tuna, and he wanted to keep talking. Talking made him feel strong and it kept Lily's touch from crushing his heart. But still, it threw him off his game enough to actually allow a little truth to seep out.

"Sometimes you resign yourself to a certain fate," he said, "but then that fate changes. It takes getting used to. I was invisible my whole life until I fell into that fish's mouth. If it hadn't have been for dumb luck, I'd still be invisible."

"I don't think it was dumb luck," Lily said. "In the very beginning, when God created the universe, He also created the big fish. He made you invisible to keep you safe, so that one day you could both meet."

"You might speak the truth," Jonah lied.

"You were saved, so Nineveh could be saved, and maybe also," she continued trepidatiously, "so we could now be talking."

She had failed to tally into her equation Vito, who sat chewing his sleeve pensively.

"Maybe God," Vito thought, "originally sent down an angel to push my hand toward Jonah's penis. Or maybe the angel pulled Jonah's penis toward my hand. Maybe, sometimes, when it is a matter of great historical importance, angels are allowed to step in—to halt a sacrifice, to guide the mouth of a fish, to move a hand toward a penis. Anything is possible in this great circus of a universe."

Vito listened to Jonah and Lily talk. He was about to interrupt, but decided better of it.

"If the complete fool is prophet," he thought, "then the kid's got to be at least half an oracle."

And then, like his mother, his father, and God in Heaven, he leaned back and watched in silence.

My Troubles
(A Work in Progress,
by Joseph of N—)

The thing with pregnant women is that they glow. I know you've heard this—how they walk around like uranium buddhas spreading joy and light; but the way my Mary glowed was for real. Mary was like the sunrise, and when she smiled her kind little smile, you had to literally shield your eyes.

Another thing about pregnant women, or at least it's something I've noticed with Mary, is that they're supremely confident, like their bellies are puffed-out barrel chests and they're looking for a tussle, but a tussle that will end in bear hugs. Because not only are they confident, but they're filled with love. Mary sometimes calls me over while I'm sanding a chair or something and just quietly strokes the side of my face.

"You're okay?" she asks.

"Of course I'm okay," I say. "I'm the one who should be asking if you're okay."

But of course I know what she's getting at.

"How's the holy baby?" Ezekiel, my foreman at work, asks me, like, ten times a day, and I have no choice but to bite it. It's either that or be out of a job. And that's the last thing I need right now. On top of everything else, can you imagine me, Mary, and the kid losing the house and having to live in a tree? Living off cranberries and pomegranate seeds like a tree rodent? No, thanks.

Being chosen by the Lord is an honor. I'm not saying it's not, and objectively speaking, I know it like I know anything else. It's flattering to think that your girl-friend is good enough for God, and on some days I can convince myself well enough that it is an honor indeed, but if the guys at work don't act like it's an honor, and none of your friends or family acts like it's an honor, then it doesn't feel so much like an honor. And so you end up just feeling like your garden-variety guy who's been cheated on. Sure, you've been cheated on with the Lord, but still.

231

I should also say that even getting to the point where I *believed* Mary was an ulcer wrapped in a hernia. She had never lied to me before and I knew her heart like I knew my own, but when she told me this business about being visited by an angel, I had an honest-to-God conniption. Stomach pains. Fistfuls of chest hair. Rending the clothes from my back—trying to shove our dining table through the front door. You name it.

"Is that the best you can come up with?" I asked. "Don't you have enough respect for me to create something a little less . . . I don't know . . . completely insane?"

When I got this way—"up to my tricks" is what she called it—Mary would make herself into a wall. The crazier I got, the wallier she got. Our fights were like a game of handball. I'd throw at her everything I had just to break through, to make an impression, and it would just bounce off. I'd say things I didn't mean, stupid, wrathful things that even didn't make sense.

"Sister, thou art the cracked egg that hath hatched a chicken of lies."

I would wave my unlovableness right up in her face, and she'd stare through it as though in a dream. My dad used to call Mary The Sleepwalker. She acted like she was sleeping while she ate, while she worked, while she was spoken to.

"She's just sensitive to things we can't see," I'd say in her defense.

My dad could never understand what I saw in her; but what my dad never stopped to think about was what exactly Mary saw in *me*. You see, to most I was a high-strung whiner, but to Mary, all of my whining was a laugh riot.

"What's up with coconuts? I almost dislocated my shoulder pummeling one of the s.o.b.'s against a rock—and for what? To drink coconut milk? Yech. The least God could have done was fill them with pineapple juice."

When I complained, Mary would shake her head and laugh like I was the funniest guy in the world. So as whiny and annoying as I'd get, there was always Mary, giggling away like it was all a big act, like underneath it all, there was a nice funny heart that deserved to be loved. On most days her love was enough to make me feel like a pretty big man.

But after a whole night of screaming and crying, I don't think she was finding me such a laugh-a-minute.

I went outside to try and cool off. Sitting on a tree stump, I felt a hand on my shoulder. I turned around and there he was: an angel. The whole bit. Wings and everything, just squatting there. Talk about a lack of stagecraft. I almost went back to chewing on my knuckle skin and ignoring him entirely.

"Are you the one . . . with Mary?" I asked, not looking at him.

"No," he said softly. "I just came here to tell you that what Mary tells you is the truth."

"This is a lot to digest," I said. The angel withdrew his hand from my shoulder and left me sitting there outside my house, digesting until morning.

Even after all that, I was still a mess.

"What did the angel look like?" I would ask every so often.

"What difference does that make?" she'd say, laughing.

"I just want to know," I'd say.

In the early days, I was all about the little details. What was he wearing? What did he say to you? Was he a handsome angel? What do you mean there was a blinding flash of heavenly light? And what about my light? Would you describe my light as heavenly? But after a while I started to feel like a fool. I mean, for God's sake, being jealous of an angel!

So it was pretty soon afterward that I started to worry. The angels must have seen Mary from Heaven and knew she was the right one for the job, but they probably didn't get a very good look at me. While they were all lying around on the clouds mooning over Mary, they probably missed her loudmouth boyfriend in the background griping about his stubbed toe. Who was I to be raising an angel baby? What could I teach a baby of any kind? How to hyperventilate when you're outbid for a carpentry job? How to cry in frustration when your roof caves in? What kid is going to want to hang around with me? All I have to teach him is how to worry. That was an area in which I excelled.

And worry I did—worry that the baby might not even look like people, that he might be born with wings. Or worse, be born with just one wing. The thought of Mary holding a one-winged baby on her lap was enough to get me all weepy and sick to my stomach. If that son of a bitch Ezekiel made even one little crack about my illegitimate one-winged baby, job or no job, I'd strangle him with my bare hands.

Now the very last thing I needed in the midst of all this was to load up the mule and take Mary and myself out of town for a census. The Romans were obsessed with counting things—as though numbers offered you a glimpse at the greater truths in life—and so everyone had to pack up and be counted in their city of birth, which, for Mary and me, was Bethlehem.

What a sight! The two of us hobbling along on a mule. Did you know that a mule is the offspring of a horse and a donkey? It's a hybrid. Like, say, the way a Pegasus is a hybrid—the offspring of a horse and, I'm guessing, an eagle. Now can you imagine how that Pegasus's horse mother's horse husband felt when that eagle first swooped down with roses and sweet talk? Do you see what I'm getting at here?

When we got to Bethlehem, it was like everyone and their uncle Nimrod was there. Every place in town was booked. On the edge of the city, we found a little dive, and it was there, exhausted after a day of refusals, that I decided that I simply wasn't going to take no for an answer. Mary saw how I was getting—the stress vein on my forehead two seconds from bursting—and so she kept telling me how everything was going to be okay, but of course, when you're living half in a dream, frolicking with the angels, you can sleep on a mule, on a daisy—on the head of a pin; me, I deal with cold hard reality, and if I couldn't even get a lousy bed for us, what kind of a job would I do for Mary and the kid? If those angels up there thought I was good for anything at all, it was maybe at the very least that I was a hustler—that I was the kind of guy who would provide—keep her safe. But it looked like I couldn't even do that much.

A little bearded man greeted us at the door. Right off the bat, he raised his hand, blocking me. No dice, he said.

"Listen," I said, putting half my body through the door frame, "you have to have something. Do you know what kind of a journey we had? I have a pregnant woman here."

I was tempted to tell him a few more things—about the angels and the hybrid on the way—but he just looked over my shoulder at Mary on the mule, her face tilted up at the sky, her eyes unblinking, and he took pity on us. I wasn't crazy about getting by on pity, but it was getting late.

He handed us a blanket and said we could stay in his stable. A stable. The word was like a gob of spit dripping off my eyelashes. Tears of rage burned my throat. A stable! I'd worked my whole life only to have my wife give birth to an angel baby in a lousy manger.

Inside the stable the animals were completely silent. Not asleep, just quiet. I don't know if you've ever been in a room full of silent animals, but it's eerie and unnatural. I looked at them and they looked back at me, silently judging me.

"You know," said Mary in the quiet, "I really feel like things are going to be different somehow after this baby is born."

"That's the way it goes," I said, clumping up some hay for us. "My dad used to say that, too. After the kids are born, he'd say, nothing is ever the same again."

"I just feel," Mary went on, "that this is a very special kid we've got here."

"All mothers feel that way," I said.

"I know," she said.

"Looking at you in this stable, I could just punch myself in the face," I said.

Mary reached out and rubbed my cheek. She did it like she always did. Like an old man. Her hand was warm.

"I'm just so happy you're here," she whispered.

"I know," I said. I wanted to ask if she thought the baby might somehow look like me, just a little bit—to keep things smooth at work—but I figured I'd hold off.

I turned over onto my stomach and Mary started in on the knots in my back. As she rubbed, I complained and told her my worries, and as I complained she laughed and the sound of Mary's laughter was like angels' wings clapping. For the first time in a long time, it felt like things were going to be okay.

In about three minutes I'd be asleep, and sometime after that Mary would be, too, her head resting on my back. The thing with me and Mary is that whenever we fall asleep, somehow, in the middle of the night, we end up holding hands. And that night in the stable, when Mary woke in the darkness with a sudden start, like always, our fingers were entwined. And when Mary squeezed my hand, I sprang into action.